SAMANTHA
An American Girl Holiday

TELESCRIPT BY MARSHA NORMAN

Based on the books by Valerie Tripp,
Susan S. Adler, and Maxine Rose Schur

Photography by Brooke Palmer and Peter Stranks
Editorial development by Tamara England
Designed by Francesca Piuma
Produced by Paula Moon-Bailey, Richmond Powers, Jeannette Bailey, and Judith Lary

TABLE OF CONTENTS

INTRODUCTION

Turning a book into a movie is a big job. Shaping the six Samantha books into a two-hour movie required cutting, rewriting, and adding story elements. As you read this script, you'll see that many scenes are much like they were written in the Samantha books. You'll also find that some parts of the books have been left out, while new scenes have been added—scenes that take advantage of a visually beautiful setting, scenes that have been added to increase drama, and smaller scenes that provide transition from one major scene to another. Characters have been left out or changed. Settings have changed, and even the order of events has shifted to match the rhythm and pacing of movie storytelling.

More changes can occur even after the script is finished, so there may be some differences between this script and the final movie. That's because during rehearsal and filming, the director may decide that a shift of action or dialogue is necessary for the flow of the movie. Still other changes can happen when the movie is *edited*, or put together from beginning to end.

Even with these shifts, cuts, and additions, the story of Samantha Parkington, a girl growing up at the turn of the twentieth century— a girl longing for a family of her own—shines through the pages of this script. As you read the script to yourself or act it out with friends, see if you can find where things vary from the books. And then see if you can figure out why the screenwriter and the director decided to make the changes that were made.

But most of all, enjoy watching Samantha Parkington and her family and friends brought to life in a whole new way!

The Cast

SAMANTHA   *AnnaSophia Robb*

GRANDMARY Mia Farrow

UNCLE GARD   *Jordan Bridges*

AUNT CORNELIA   Rebecca Mader

NELLIE   Kelsey Lewis

JENNY   Olivia Ballantyne

BRIDGET   Hannah Endicott-Douglas

EDDIE   Michael Kanev

ABBREVIATIONS USED
IN THE TELESCRIPT

CAM   camera

CONT.   continued

CU   close-up

EXT.   exterior

INT.   interior

O.S.   off-screen (active dialogue by a speaker
           who is not shown on-screen)

P.O.V.   point of view (the position from which
           the action is being seen)

V.O.   voice-over (voicing unspoken thoughts
           of a character who is on-screen)

Note: Gaps in the numbering of the scenes are due to
the omission of some scenes during filming.

The Script

ACT ONE

1   EXT. A GORGEOUS GREEN LAWN – DAY
A happy bright-eyed, girl runs toward the camera. She is SAMANTHA, age 9.

From off-screen, we hear the voice of a young boy.

>   EDDIE RYLAND (O.S.)
>   Samantha!

2   TITLE CARD COMES UP: LATE SPRING 1904, MOUNT BEDFORD, NEW YORK
SAMANTHA climbs up a tree and arrives at a crook, where she settles into her favorite spot.

Below her, a boy races up to the tree. He is EDDIE RYLAND.

>   EDDIE RYLAND
>   Samantha!

Samantha grins from her perch.

>   EDDIE RYLAND
>   You're so dumb you probably think three
>   times four is twelve.

>   SAMANTHA
>   Three times four *is* twelve, Eddie.

That stops him.

> SAMANTHA
> If you don't leave me alone, I'll find your
> money jar and empty it in the river!

> EDDIE
> You're too dumb to find it.

> SAMANTHA
> Eddie Ryland, you—!

As she moves to reach for a far branch, she loses her balance and falls. Eddie laughs. She dusts herself off and chases him across the lawn.

> SAMANTHA
> Come back here!!

She catches up to him quickly and then they both STOP SHORT.

3   EXT. DRIVEWAY – DAY
A FAMILY approaches – a kind-looking, handsome Irish man and his three daughters, ages 9, 7, and 5.

Samantha's eyes light up at the prospect of girls next door.

> SAMANTHA
> Who are they?

> EDDIE RYLAND
> *(imperious and nasty)*
> They're our new servants. The big one is my
> new maid.

SAMANTHA
She's too young to be a maid. Maybe her
mother is the maid.

The oldest girl, NELLIE, carries two carpetbags. The little girls are both miserable.

NELLIE'S FATHER
(affectionately)
Come along now, Bridget.

BRIDGET
I'm tired, Da.

NELLIE'S FATHER (O.S.)
I know.

NELLIE
(arm around the youngest girl)
And I know you're hungry, Jenny, but you'll
just have to wait.

Samantha backs up a little, watching as . . .

A HOUSEKEEPER greets them and takes them around the back. Samantha follows, eager to see what will happen next.

4   EXT. CARRIAGE HOUSE – DAY

As the housekeeper talks to Nellie's father, the girls wait patiently.

Samantha comes around the corner of the house.

Samantha spies Eddie Ryland slinking along the ground, slingshot in hand. He aims and . . .

NELLIE

Owwww!

A pebble bounces off Nellie and breaks a small window above her. Eddie races up to her.

EDDIE RYLAND

See what you did.

NELLIE

I didn't do nuthin'.

EDDIE RYLAND

You threw a rock and broke a window. And
I'm going to tell unless you give me a penny.

NELLIE

I don't have a penny.

Samantha comes up now, to back up Nellie.

SAMANTHA

She's not paying you a cent, Eddie Ryland.
And if you make any more trouble, I'll tell
your mother you took her good petticoat and
made a kite's tail out of it.

Nellie's father comes back now and takes the bags up the carriage house steps.

EDDIE RYLAND

Oh, I'm really scared, Samantha!

From the porch, Eddie's mother calls out to him.

MRS. RYLAND

Edward. I have an errand for you.

He runs off.

NELLIE

Thank you, Miss.

SAMANTHA

I'm Samantha. *(curtsies)* I live next door.

NELLIE

I'm Nellie, and this is Jenny and Bridget.

BRIDGET

Pleased to meet you.

SAMANTHA
(leans in)
Don't pay any attention to him.

NELLIE

Have to pay some attention, miss, if we want
to keep our place here.

NELLIE'S FATHER

Nellie girl, come along now.

But Samantha doesn't want to let her go.

SAMANTHA

Are you going to Mount Bedford School?
Maybe we'll be in the same class.

NELLIE

I don't go to school, miss. We're here to work.

Nellie starts up the steps. Samantha keeps talking.

SAMANTHA
May I see you tomorrow?

NELLIE
Like I said, I'll be workin', miss. From the size
of this place, from dawn to dusk.

Samantha has never heard anybody talk like this. As Nellie walks away, Sam hears the cook looking for her.

MRS. HAWKINS
Samantha? Samantha!

SAMANTHA
Good-bye, Nellie. Good-bye, Bridget. Good-
bye, Jenny.

Samantha runs through the hedges, across the lawn, and toward the steps to the kitchen entrance of Grandmary's house.

5   EXT. GRANDMARY'S PORCH – MOMENTS LATER
SAMANTHA rushes toward the steps. She can't wait to share her news with MRS. HAWKINS, the cook, and JESSIE, the maid.

SAMANTHA
The Rylands have new servants. A father and
three girls. One of them is my age!

MRS. HAWKINS
Samantha, look at those stockings. Your
grandmother won't like that, no, she won't.

                         SAMANTHA
              Yes, Mrs. Hawkins.

Samantha turns toward the door. The women watch her go.

                        MRS. HAWKINS
              Be sure to wash your hands, now.

                         SAMANTHA
              Yes, Mrs. Hawkins.

                          JESSIE
                    (crosses herself)
              She's just like her mother.

                        MRS. HAWKINS
              And growing more like her by the day.

6   INT. THE HALLWAY – DAY
Samantha stops for a moment in front of the mirror. She wipes the dirt from her face and hands. She looks down to see if there is a way to hide the torn stocking. Then she bolts for the parlor. The CLOCK STARTS TO CHIME.

AT THE DOOR OF THE PARLOR, Samantha stops, smooths her hair in place, and walks quickly into the parlor, eyes down, as if she were calm as can be.

7   INT. THE PARLOR – DAY
GRANDMARY sits in a chair, working on a piece of embroidery. As the clock strikes four, Samantha sits down at the piano.

                        GRANDMARY
              Hello, Samantha.

SAMANTHA

Hello, Grandmary.

GRANDMARY

I trust you have a good explanation for the tear in your stockings.

SAMANTHA

I fell. I'm sorry.

GRANDMARY

You weren't running, were you?

SAMANTHA

Not when I fell, no.

GRANDMARY

Haste makes waste, Samantha.

SAMANTHA

Yes, Grandmary. *(pause)* Did you know? There are three—

GRANDMARY

You can tell me over tea, dear. Begin, please, Samantha.

SAMANTHA

—three girls moving in next door, and one of them is my age!

GRANDMARY

Samantha . . . begin please.

Samantha begins playing, beautifully. The music carries us through the room. We see beautiful tapestries and an oil painting of a little girl (somewhat resembling Samantha) and a little boy.

As Grandmary's eyes drift over to the painting, Jessie enters with the mail.

JESSIE
(whispering)
The afternoon mail is here, Mrs. Edwards.

GRANDMARY
Just put it on the table, Jessie.

Samantha continues playing but strains to see the mail.

SAMANTHA
Is there a letter from Uncle Gard?

GRANDMARY
We'll open the mail later, dear.

SAMANTHA
But is he coming back when he said? He didn't
miss the boat, did he?

GRANDMARY
Finish your practice, please.

Reluctantly, Samantha turns back to the piano. Then she looks up and out the window.

7   SAMANTHA'S P.O.V. – OUT THE WINDOW – DAY
Sam sees Eddie Ryland flying a kite with a long tail. Nellie comes out of her house wearing a maid's uniform.

10   EXT. THE FRONT YARD – DAY
Nellie is hanging out clothes. Samantha comes up to her.

NELLIE

Hello, miss.

SAMANTHA

Please don't call me "miss."

NELLIE

Get in trouble if I don't, miss.

Nellie returns to work. Samantha, feeling very bold, follows her.

SAMANTHA

Where did you come from? Before Mount
Bedford, I mean.

NELLIE

New York City.

SAMANTHA

My Uncle Gard lives in New York City.

NELLIE

My da and I worked in a factory there.

SAMANTHA

You worked in a factory?

NELLIE

Yes. But Da thought we'd be better off livin'
in the country now.

Samantha understands what Nellie means. She is careful.

SAMANTHA
Is your mother . . . ?

Nellie is matter-of-fact about this, but not without feeling. Nellie just says what is.

NELLIE
She died, miss. Last winter. I want to grow up
to be just like her. Da says I look like her, in
my eyes.

Nellie takes out more washing. Samantha fingers her locket.

SAMANTHA
If you don't go to school, would you like to
borrow some of my books?

NELLIE
Wouldn't do no good, miss. Less they're all
pictures.

SAMANTHA
(the truth dawning on her)
Oh.

NELLIE
My mother was going to teach me to read,
but . . .

SAMANTHA
I could teach you! We could meet every day,
beside the hedge—

NELLIE
I wish I could, Miss.

SAMANTHA

You can. You can bring some work with you,
like darning or mending, can't you? You have
to sit down sometime. And I can sit with you.
It isn't hard to learn.

NELLIE

I'll ask my da.

11 INT. THE PARLOR – NIGHT, LATER
Grandmary and Samantha are doing needlepoint. Jessie brings in a wrapped package and leaves it on the table.

GRANDMARY

Thank you, Jessie.

SAMANTHA

Jessie?

Jessie turns.

JESSIE

Yes, miss?

SAMANTHA

How old were you when you first started
working as a maid?

Grandmary gives Samantha a stern look.

JESSIE

Would you like anything, ma'am?

23

GRANDMARY
No, thank you, Jessie. That will be all.

Jessie leaves the parlor. Samantha can feel the lecture coming. She concentrates fully on her needlepoint.

GRANDMARY
Samantha.

SAMANTHA
Yes?

GRANDMARY
We don't discuss personal matters with the servants.

SAMANTHA
In the kitchen we talk about all sorts of—

GRANDMARY
This is not the kitchen. The secret to a happy household is for everyone to know their place. Do you understand?

SAMANTHA
Yes, Grandmary.

GRANDMARY
Good. Are you enjoying your needlepoint?

SAMANTHA
Yes, Grandmary.

GRANDMARY
Then I'm sure you'd have no interest in this
package that's addressed to you.

Samantha looks up, thrilled.

SAMANTHA
(reading)
It's from Uncle Gard! How could it get here
before he did? He's not due for three weeks.

*Mrs. Hawkins and Jessie peer in from the doorway, full of curiosity, as Samantha tears into
the package and finds a STEREOPTICON.*

SAMANTHA
What is it?

She starts fiddling around with it.

GRANDMARY
It's a stereopticon. Your very own.

Samantha reads the note from Uncle Gard.

SAMANTHA
He says, "Put in the first slide," and I will see
where he is right now.

She puts the slide in, and then holds the stereopticon up to her eyes.

INSERT: IMAGE OF THE EIFFEL TOWER.

SAMANTHA
Paris! The Eiffel Tower.

Pull back to see that we are now:

12   EXT. AT THE TREE – DAY
Nellie takes the stereopticon down from her eyes.

                              NELLIE
              As if we're really there.

                            SAMANTHA
              Uncle Gard always gives me the best presents.
              He's taking me to the Exposition in St. Louis
              for a whole week in July. We're going to see
              Japanese pagodas and temples, and eat
              peanut butter and fairy floss and everything.

                              NELLIE
              They make butter out of peanuts?

                            SAMANTHA
              That's what Uncle Gard says.

                              NELLIE
              What's fairy floss?

                            SAMANTHA
              Uncle Gard says it's made of pink sugar and
              comes on a stick. Uncle Gard is the best person
              I know.

                              NELLIE
              Better'n your mam and pa?

Samantha is suddenly quiet.

                              NELLIE
              I'm sorry. Did I say somethin'?

SAMANTHA
We should start your reading lesson.

NELLIE
I'm sorry if I hurt your feelings, miss.

Samantha has never told anyone this before:

SAMANTHA
My parents are gone. Like your mother. Only in an accident. On the river.

NELLIE
Both of them? That's awful. I don't know what I'd do without my da.

SAMANTHA
(opens her locket)
Want to see them?

NELLIE
She's beautiful. And he's so handsome. You've got his hair. And your ma's eyes.

SAMANTHA
She used to sing to me. Sometimes I try to hear her voice. but it just slips away.

NELLIE
I know.

SAMANTHA
I wish I could ask Grandmary, but speaking
about Mother hurts her too much.
(*nods, referring to necklace*)
I keep them close this way.
(*Nellie smiles, comforting*)
I like that you're here, Nellie. I think we're
going to be great friends.

NELLIE
(*shyly*)
I don't have a real friend, outside of my family.

SAMANTHA
You do now, Nellie O'Malley. Friends forever.

They smile, and we know a real change has begun.

NELLIE
Forever!

13 EXT. ALONG THE SHORE OF THE RIVER – DAY
The girls walk along the shore. Nellie has a book in her hand. Samantha is pointing out the letters.

15 EXT. RYLAND HOUSE – ANOTHER DAY
Jenny and Bridget sit on the porch winding yarn with each other. Nellie supervises from the lawn while beating a rug. Samantha watches.

Jenny tangles the yarn.

                              BRIDGET
            Stop your fidgeting, Jenny!

                              NELLIE
            Bridget! You're pulling too hard on her. Wind
            slower.

                              SAMANTHA
                            (whispering)
            Why doesn't Jenny talk?

Making sure the girls can't hear.

                              NELLIE
            Hasn't said a word since Mam died.

                              SAMANTHA
            Did she talk before that?

                              NELLIE
            Some. And she talks in her sleep.

She laughs and beats the rug.

                              SAMANTHA
            That looks fun.

                              NELLIE
            It does?

                              SAMANTHA
            Can I try it? I'll beat the rug and you read.

Exchanging the book for the broom, Samantha whomps the rug.

NELLIE

Cat—

(Samantha whomps the rug)

Sat—

(whomp)

Mat—

SAMANTHA
(another wallop)

Good. Go on.

Samantha starts beating faster. She makes us laugh.

NELLIE

Fat—

(whomp)

Rat—

(whomp)

Hat—

(whomp)

Nellie laughs and laughs at the fun Samantha is having.

SAMANTHA

Scat, fat rat!

She hits the rug so hard she falls down in a cloud of dust. Nellie joins her on the ground. They laugh and laugh. Nellie's da comes up to them. He coughs as he's coming up.

NELLIE'S FATHER
You girls about through killin' the rug?

They sit up.

SAMANTHA
Sorry, Mr. O'Malley. It was my fault.

NELLIE'S FATHER
No fault to it. Ya almost done, here?

NELLIE
All done, Da.

NELLIE'S FATHER
Good then, get a move on inside. Mrs. Ryland
was calling for you.

NELLIE
Yes, Da. Tomorrow, Samantha?

SAMANTHA
Tomorrow.

Nellie gets up, brushes herself off, and leaves.

As she leaves:

NELLIE'S FATHER
I want to thank ya, Samantha, for your kindness toward Nellie, and the girls.

SAMANTHA
No need for thanks, sir. Nellie and the girls
are my friends.

Suddenly, we hear a HORN HONK. Samantha practically jumps straight up in the air.

She runs to the front yard.

SAMANTHA

It's Uncle Gard!
                (to Mr. O'Malley)
That's my Uncle Gard! He's come back from
Europe.
                (running)
Good-bye, Mr. O'Malley. Good-bye, Jenny,
Bridget. My Uncle Gard is here!

16   EXT. FRONT OF THE HOUSE – DAY

Uncle Gard's fantastic automobile drives up and stops at the curb. GARD himself, a turn-of-the-century character complete with wild tie, gets down from the car and races to meet Samantha. He takes off his duster, his cap, and his goggles. We see that nearby, Eddie Ryland is watching, holding his bicycle.

SAMANTHA
                (yelling as she comes)
Uncle Gard!!!

He scoops her up in his arms.

UNCLE GARD

My angel!

SAMANTHA

I've missed you so much!

UNCLE GARD

I missed *you* so much. Did you get my
present?

SAMANTHA

I love it. It's wonderful.

UNCLE GARD

I have an even bigger surprise for you after
supper. Just wait!

SAMANTHA

What is it?

UNCLE GARD

If I told you, it wouldn't be a surprise.

She laughs with glee. He holds her close.

SAMANTHA

Will you take me for a ride now?

UNCLE GARD takes her around the bend to his car.

UNCLE GARD

First I want you to say hello to someone.

*In the car is CORNELIA, a beautiful red-haired young woman removing her duster and
goggles. Uncle Gard drops Samantha's hand and rushes to take the duster and goggles.
He brushes a hair from Cornelia's face. For just a moment he cradles her cheek in his hand.*

*SAMANTHA NOTICES. And she's not happy. Cornelia notices Eddie as she descends
from the car.*

UNCLE GARD

Samantha, you remember Miss Pitt, from
Christmas?

CORNELIA

Please, call me Cornelia.

                    SAMANTHA
Hello.

She turns quickly back to her beloved Uncle Gard.

                    SAMANTHA
Can we go now?

                    UNCLE GARD
                    (laughing)
In a moment.

                    CORNELIA
Your Uncle Gard says you love to read, Sam.

                    SAMANTHA
My name is Samantha.

                    CORNELIA
Very well, Samantha.
                    (produces a book)
I thought you might like this.
                    (hands the book to her)
The Wizard of Oz. Girls in New York love it.

Samantha takes the book, doing her best to be polite.

                    SAMANTHA
Thank you.

Gard takes Cornelia's arm and Samantha's hand, ushering them toward the gate.

                    UNCLE GARD
Come on, you two.

SAMANTHA
But I thought we were going for a ride.

UNCLE GARD
First we need to say hello to your Grandmary.

Samantha smiles. Gard now offers an arm to each one.

UNCLE GARD
Shall we?

They both accompany him, with the slightest tug-of-war.

17 INT. THE PARLOR – DAY
On hearing the noise coming toward her, Grandmary stands.

Gard strides into the room. He is debonair and sassy and wonderful. He has Cornelia and Samantha on either side.

UNCLE GARD
Mother. You remember Miss Pitt?

GRANDMARY
What a pleasant surprise. How are you,
Miss Pitt?

CORNELIA
Very well, thank you, Mrs. Edwards. Gardner
promised me he would tell you I was coming.
I can see he didn't.

UNCLE GARD
I like surprises. Don't you, Samantha?

Samantha's silence speaks volumes.

> GRANDMARY
> *(after a moment)*
> I'm sure we'll have time to catch up later,
> Miss Pitt, but for now Mrs. Hawkins will
> show you to the guest room.

Mrs. Hawkins nods and waits for Cornelia.

> CORNELIA
> Thank you.

After Cornelia has gone:

> UNCLE GARD
> You look well, Mother. This is for you.

Uncle Gard hands Grandmary a hat box.

> GRANDMARY
> *(taking the box and starting to open it)*
> Gardner, thank you. But you really should
> warn me when you're bringing guests.
> *(taking out a hat)*
> Oh, it's lovely!

> UNCLE GARD
> Has the Admiral been to see you lately?

> GRANDMARY
> Oh, stop it, Gardner.

She looks her beloved son over.

                    GRANDMARY
          You're far too thin.

                    UNCLE GARD
          See what happens without Mrs. Hawkins's
          cookies?

Uncle Gard looks down at Samantha, as if confused.

                    UNCLE GARD
          Let's see. We were going to do something
          now . . .

                    GRANDMARY
          What?

                    UNCLE GARD
          I don't remember.

Samantha shrieks with joy and runs back outside, pulling Gard out.

                    UNCLE GARD
          Excuse us, Mother!

                    GRANDMARY
          Where are you going? Gard?!

18A EXT. GARD'S CAR – AFTERNOON
     Samantha and Gard drive along a country road, Samantha exhilarated and full of joy.

GRANDMARY
You were away an awfully long time. How
did the firm manage without you?

UNCLE GARD
I don't think they even noticed I'd gone
away!

CORNELIA
Oh, nonsense, Gardner. Of course they did.

UNCLE GARD
You know, Cornelia is the one who's really
making a difference in New York.

GRANDMARY
Is that true? How so?

UNCLE GARD
She is organizing suffrage meetings all over
the city.

CORNELIA
Gard, perhaps this isn't the best time to—

GRANDMARY
I don't understand why women need to vote.
Women of my generation have found plenty
of ways to influence decisions—without having
to stand on a soapbox.

CORNELIA

Yes, that is certainly true. Although . . . if
women are expected to obey the laws our
leaders make, shouldn't we have a say in
selecting those leaders?
(now looking at Samantha)
I believe Samantha should have as much say
in her government as that little boy from next
door.

A disapproving look from Grandmary.

SAMANTHA
(interrupting)
Uncle Gard, when are you going to tell us the
surprise?

UNCLE GARD

Well, I was going to wait until . . .

SAMANTHA

Are you coming to live in Mount Bedford?

UNCLE GARD

No. But it *is* the most wonderful news!
(walks to Cornelia)
Against her better judgment, this beautiful
woman has accepted my proposal of marriage.

Samantha is stricken. She thought surprises were good.

CORNELIA
(laughing)
Oh, Gardner, you sound so old-fashioned. We've
been talking about this for almost a year.

UNCLE GARD
And while I was in Paris, I was getting her
parents' blessing.

Grandmary stiffens.

GRANDMARY
Well, then, I'm happy for both of you.

Grandmary gives Samantha a look. Samantha manages a small smile.

SAMANTHA
I'm happy for you too, Uncle Gard.

UNCLE GARD
Since Cornelia's family lives abroad, I hope
you will allow us to have the wedding right
here. We could hold it in the conservatory!

CORNELIA
It's so beautiful here.

UNCLE GARD
We were thinking the end of July.

SAMANTHA
(reacts to the word)
July?

GRANDMARY
Of this year?

CORNELIA
Well, yes . . .

UNCLE GARD

Of course, this year.

GRANDMARY

Why so sudden?

UNCLE GARD

I don't want to wait! I've found the woman of
my dreams.

Samantha flinches.

GRANDMARY

But it's the beginning of May. We haven't
announced your engagement, or given a
dinner . . .

UNCLE GARD

We'll have three months to have dinners. As
many dinners as you want. And then we can
take our honeymoon in August and be back
by September.

CORNELIA

I want you to be a bridesmaid, Samantha.
Would you? I mean, if that's all right with
you, Mrs. Edwards.

GRANDMARY

She's a little young . . .

CORNELIA

Well, my sister will be my matron of honor,
and her daughter, my flower girl. But I don't
have a bridesmaid. What do you say?

UNCLE GARD
                    Say yes.

Everyone looks to Samantha to break the tension and to acquiesce.

                              SAMANTHA
                    Yes.

*A little dubious, she looks around the table, her heart about to break. She takes a moment
and forces herself to act like a lady, even though her feelings are in a most unladylike
tumult.*

                            END OF ACT ONE

42

ACT TWO

21 EXT. RYLANDS' HOUSE – BACKYARD – MORNING
Nellie looks around, wondering where Samantha is.

> NELLIE
> *(loud whisper toward the hedges)*
> Samantha? Samantha?

No answer. She goes back to work.

24 EXT. GRANDMARY'S HOUSE – MORNING
Uncle Gard searches the garden. He finally sees Samantha down by the water, sitting alone. He walks up to her.

> UNCLE GARD
> Samantha?

> SAMANTHA
> Hello.

Uncle Gard sits down beside her.

> UNCLE GARD
> I know you're upset with me, and I should
> have known better than to surprise you and
> Mother.

> SAMANTHA
> I don't want things to change any more,
> Uncle Gard.

UNCLE GARD

Dear sweet girl, you have had more change
in your life than anyone ought to have. But,
you'll see, Cornelia is going to be a wonderful
friend. In fact, if your mother were alive, I'm
sure they'd be the best of friends.

SAMANTHA

They would?

UNCLE GARD

Oh, yes, they're quite similar in many ways—
your mother was full of life and questions
and causes. I'm sure she's smiling on us right
now . . .

SAMANTHA

. . . and making fun of your bushy eyebrows . . .

UNCLE GARD

How did you know about that?

SAMANTHA

She tortured you. She told me so.

UNCLE GARD

Every day. And I miss her every time I think
of it. You are so like your mother. You have
her spirit. You have her will and her curiosity.

Samantha is miles away. Uncle Gard looks at her, then at the stereopticon. UNCLE GARD

What's this?
                    (he looks)
St. Louis? The Exposition.

44

UNCLE GARD(CONT.)
(*realization*)
Oh, no . . . I promised to take you, didn't I?

Samantha nods.

UNCLE GARD
I'm so sorry. How can I make it up to you?
There's so much else happening . . .
I completely forgot.

SAMANTHA
It's all *her* fault.

UNCLE GARD
No. No, Samantha. You mustn't think that.
Cornelia is a wonderful person, she's strong
and caring, she loves children . . .

SAMANTHA
You'll have your own family and forget all
about me.

UNCLE GARD
You'll always be my family . . . my little girl.
But you must give Cornelia a chance.

Samantha looks at him.

UNCLE GARD
Please?

SAMANTHA
All right, Uncle Gard. I will.

They hug.

25   INT. PARLOR – 2 WEEKS LATER

CAM follows the music to Samantha practicing. She finishes the piece.

> GRANDMARY
>
> That was lovely.

> SAMANTHA
>
> Thank you, Grandmary.

Samantha gets up to leave.

> SAMANTHA
>
> Grandmary?

> GRANDMARY
>
> Yes, Samantha.

> SAMANTHA
>
> Do you like Cornelia?

> GRANDMARY
>
> Do I—
>
> > *(carefully)*
>
> Certainly I do, Samantha. She's going to be
> Gardner's wife and your aunt. Our family.
>
> > *(gently)*
>
> Much as we'd like things to remain as they
> are, Samantha, they don't. And so we must
> learn to accept change with grace. Do you
> understand?

> SAMANTHA
>
> Yes, Grandmary.

27A EXT. UNDER THE HEDGES – DAY

Sam and Nellie have a reading lesson at the hedge. Nellie closes the book.

> NELLIE
> "... Flopsy, Mopsy, and Cotton-tail had
> bread and milk and blackberries for supper.
> The End."

> SAMANTHA
> I can't believe how quickly you learned this,
> Nellie.

> NELLIE
> I think I've been readin' over Da's shoulders
> ever since I was little. He says I should start
> teachin' Bridget soon.

The hedges move a bit. Samantha and Nellie freeze.

But the face that appears is Cornelia's.

> CORNELIA
> Hello there!

> NELLIE
> I should get back to work.

> CORNELIA
> Can you stay a minute longer? I'm trying to
> decide what kind of cake to have for the wed-
> ding.

Cornelia produces two little cakes.

CORNELIA
Now, then. Have a bite of both and tell me which you like better. Lemon or almond vanilla.

Nellie takes a bite of each cake. So does Samantha.

NELLIE
Ooh. I like the lemon, but the almond vanilla is wonderful, too.

CORNELIA
Maybe you'd better taste them again.

SAMANTHA
I say the lemon.

NELLIE
I have to agree.

Cornelia takes another bite of Samantha's cake.

CORNELIA
Lemon it is!

She takes the plates back.

CORNELIA
All right, then. I'll just give the rest to the dog.

NELLIE
Oh no, Ma'am, cake's not good for dogs. Gives 'em a tummy ache.

SAMANTHA
And we don't have a dog.

CORNELIA
(with a gleam in her eye)
Oh, that's right. I forgot.

SAMANTHA
Why don't we take them to Bridget and Jenny?

CORNELIA
Good idea. Very good. Thank you, girls.

She disappears as quickly as she came, leaving the cakes with the girls.

NELLIE
She's not so bad, you know.

28   INT. GRANDMARY'S HOUSE – UPSTAIRS BEDROOM – LATE AFTERNOON
Cornelia, Grandmary, Samantha, and the DRESSMAKER from New York City are looking over the wedding clothes.

GRANDMARY
Lovely!

CORNELIA
What did you wear when you got married,
Mrs. Edwards?

GRANDMARY
Belgian lace.

CORNELIA
How elegant.

GRANDMARY
The gown had tiny pearls around the trim,
with crystal beading in between each pearl.
And a large satin bow over the bustle, and . . .

SAMANTHA
(giggling)
A bustle?

GRANDMARY
(smiling)
It was quite fashionable, I'll have you know.

SAMANTHA
Tell her about the veil.

GRANDMARY
The veil—it flowed out behind like a
waterfall.

SAMANTHA
(quietly)
My mother wore it, too.

GRANDMARY
(lost in thought)
She looked like an angel.

CORNELIA
How beautiful.

The dressmaker pulls out a roll of fabric.

DRESSMAKER
And here's the fabric for the bridesmaid dress.

SAMANTHA
Ohhh, Grandmary, look! Lavender.

                    GRANDMARY
Your favorite color.

                    DRESSMAKER
Let's get some quick measurements.

The dressmaker measures Samantha.

                    SAMANTHA
It's the prettiest color I've ever seen.

                    DRESSMAKER
And it's going to look wonderful on you.

Samantha's eyes widen with delight.

29   INT. PARLOR – EVENING
Samantha walks down the stairs.

Gard and Grandmary are having an argument.

                    UNCLE GARD
Samantha had her heart set on going to
St. Louis. We have to make it up to her.
I want her to come and live with us in
New York for the fall. You said yourself
Aunt Frances is not getting any better.

Samantha arrives in the hallway by the door and overhears.

                    GRANDMARY (O.S.)
It's impossible. You'll be newly married.
The last thing you'll need is a child on your
hands.

UNCLE GARD (O.S.)
Let me share the burden, Mother. Samantha
can come and live with us. It's just for a few
months.

Samantha reacts to the word "burden."

30   EXT. THE RYLANDS' CARRIAGE HOUSE – NIGHT
Samantha walks to Nellie's door.

A pebble is thrown at a window. Samantha stands below in the dark.

SAMANTHA
(calling up)
Nellie! Nellie!

Footsteps are heard on the stairs coming down from the apartment above the carriage house.

NELLIE
(whispering)
I'm coming, I'm coming.

Samantha runs to her and grabs her.

SAMANTHA
Oh, Nellie.

NELLIE
What on earth?

SAMANTHA
(sobbing)
I tried to sleep, but I keep hearing what they
said. They think I'm a burden.

NELLIE

Who does?

SAMANTHA

They were talking about sending me away, to
New York . . . Grandmary and Uncle Gard . . .
they think I'm a burden!

Samantha dissolves into tears.

NELLIE

Look at you, you're shaking, you're so cold.
How long have you been out here?

Samantha looks around at the night again.

SAMANTHA

Please. Come with me. I don't want to be by
myself.

Nellie follows her. They walk away together.

31 EXT./INT. THE BOATHOUSE – NIGHT

Samantha runs in the door, jumps in the canoe, and covers herself with a blanket.

Nellie enters.

NELLIE

Samantha?

She hears Samantha crying.

A lamp casts a magical glow over everything. Nellie sees a whole private world that Samantha has built. There's a dollhouse, dolls, books, the stereopticon, and other little treasures that are meaningful to Samantha, such as her father's pipe and her mother's hairbrush. There are also pictures of her parents.

> NELLIE
> I thought this was just a boathouse. But it's . . .

Samantha sits up in the canoe, wrapped in the blanket, an old, soft Pendleton.

> SAMANTHA
> This is where Mother and Father and I kept
> our boat. But after they died, no one came
> anymore. Sometimes when I come here now,
> I feel like they're still here.

Samantha holds out the blanket. Nellie walks over and steps inside the canoe, then Samantha wraps both of them in the blanket.

> NELLIE
> What do you do in here?

> SAMANTHA
> Read, mostly. Make wishes.

> NELLIE
> What do you wish for?

> SAMANTHA
> It depends on my mood. Sometimes I wish
> for Eddie Ryland to run into a tree.
> *(Nellie laughs)*
> And other times I wish for my parents to be
> here.

NELLIE

My da says, no sense thinking about what you don't have. Better to think about what you do. But I still wish I could see my mam.

SAMANTHA

If I go to New York I'll miss you so much.

NELLIE

You can write to me every day!

SAMANTHA

And you can write back.

Nellie notices the Lydia doll that Samantha cradles to her.

NELLIE
(indicating the doll)
What's her name?

SAMANTHA

Lydia . . . Just like my mother.

NELLIE

I've never seen anything so beautiful.

SAMANTHA
(thinking)
If I go away, will you keep Lydia for me?

NELLIE

Do you mean it?

SAMANTHA
Yes. I wouldn't trust her with anybody but
my best friend.

Nellie clutches Lydia to her chest. She looks around.

Nellie and Samantha lean back in the canoe, propping themselves up on the big pillow.

NELLIE
You know anything about stars?

SAMANTHA
A little. First star you see, that's the wishing
one.

Through the open door they see a star.

Samantha reaches for Nellie's hand. They close their eyes and make a wish.

NELLIE AND SAMANTHA
Starlight, star bright,

first star I see tonight . . .

Wish I may, wish I might,

have the wish I wish tonight.

END OF ACT TWO

ACT THREE

32   INT. THE BOATHOUSE – MORNING
The girls awaken to the shrieks of the horrible Eddie Ryland.

> **EDDIE RYLAND**
> I found you! I found you!

> **SAMANTHA**
> You get out of here right now, Eddie.

> **EDDIE RYLAND**
> Pay me a nickel and I won't tell.

> **SAMANTHA**
> How much do you want for never speaking
> to me again?

The girls scramble up and out the door.

32A EXT. THE BOATHOUSE – MORNING

> **EDDIE RYLAND**
> *(runs up toward the house)*
> I found them! I found them!

33 EXT. THE BOATHOUSE – MORNING
At the door of the boathouse stand Mrs. Ryland, Grandmary, Gard, Nellie's father, Eddie, and Mrs. Hawkins.

MRS. RYLAND
(to Nellie)
This is completely unacceptable. The servants in my household do not trespass on other people's property, nor do they sleep outside with the neighbor's children.
(to Grandmary)
I'm so sorry. I cannot understand how this happened.

SAMANTHA
It was my fault, Mrs. Ryland. It was all my idea. I asked Nellie to keep me company.

MRS. RYLAND
Nevertheless, I expect my help to behave respectfully at all times.

GRANDMARY
I don't think the girls meant any harm.

NELLIE'S FATHER
(to Mrs. Ryland)
I promise you it won't happen again.
(then to Grandmary)
Please forgive her, Mum. She's still young, and forgets her place.

NELLIE
(to Mrs. Ryland)
I'm sorry, Ma'am. I won't do it again.
(to Grandmary)
So sorry, Ma'am. I knew better, I did.

GRANDMARY

It's all right, Nellie.

Samantha runs to Nellie and embraces her. Grandmary is transfixed by the scene. Samantha's need for a friend becomes painfully clear to her.

Uncle Gard motions to Grandmary to come look inside the boathouse.

Gard and Grandmary enter the boathouse.

UNCLE GARD

Mother.

34   INT. THE BOATHOUSE – MORNING

Stepping inside, Grandmary sees a shrine more than a broken-down boathouse. There are pictures of Samantha's parents, boxes of writing paper, etc. Samantha stands in the doorway.

GRANDMARY

What is all this?
(looking around)
Pictures of Lydia. Her shawls, her journals.
Samantha!

Samantha runs away.

Grandmary looks around. Her own memories triggered, she begins to tear up.

Uncle Gard has also picked up something of his sister's to look at, a photo, perhaps.

GRANDMARY

I've been wrong not to talk to Samantha more
about her mother.

UNCLE GARD

It's still hard for any of us to talk about Lydia.
Samantha's still grieving. Has she made any
friends?

GRANDMARY

Only the girl from next door. I think a few
months in New York will do Samantha good,
if you're sure you can manage.

UNCLE GARD

I am.

GRANDMARY

Then I'll come to New York in time for
Thanksgiving and bring Samantha back here
after Christmas.

UNCLE GARD

Good. I'm glad.

34A EXT. BY THE HEDGE – DAY
Samantha and Grandmary in conversation.

GRANDMARY

I have some wonderful news. Your Uncle Gard
has invited you to spend a few months in New
York City with him and Cornelia this fall.
(Samantha turns white)

GRANDMARY (CONT.)

And it occurred to me that with you in the city, I should probably take some time and visit your Great-Aunt Frances. She was quite ill this fall, remember? And then I'll join you in New York for the holidays.

SAMANTHA
(*suddenly*)

I'm sorry I put Mother's pictures in the boat-house.

GRANDMARY
(*quietly*)

This is not a punishment, dear. I hope it will be an adventure.

SAMANTHA

I'll never do it again. I promise, Grandmary.

GRANDMARY

My sweet child, when all we have left of someone is our memories of them, we need to keep those memories close. I'd be disappointed if you didn't have a special place for your mother. You know, she did the very same thing.

SAMANTHA

My mother?

GRANDMARY
(*nodding*)

She had a kitten named Mabel.

                    SAMANTHA
That's a funny name.

                    GRANDMARY
It was gray and fluffy, and a little cross-eyed.

                    SAMANTHA
                     (laughing)
Cross-eyed?

                    GRANDMARY
She loved that cat more than anything. And
when Mabel didn't come home one day, you
know what she did?

Samantha shakes her head no. Grandmary's eyes are full.

                 GRANDMARY (CONT.)
She put all of Mabel's favorite things—her
yarn ball, her bed, her brush—and she placed
them in the boathouse.

                    SAMANTHA
She did?

Grandmary kisses the top of Samantha's head.

                    GRANDMARY
Just. Like. You.

37   INT. GRANDMARY'S HOUSE – WEDDING DAY
      P.O.V.: Grandmary

*SAMANTHA appears at the top of the stairs in her pale lavender bridesmaid's dress, with
wide sash and hat. She looks so grown-up. It takes Grandmary's breath away.*

GRANDMARY

Samantha. Oh, my!

Grandmary holds her arms out. Samantha runs down the stairs.

SAMANTHA

Isn't it the most wonderful gown you've ever
seen, Grandmary?

GRANDMARY

The most wonderful. I was just on my way to
see Cornelia. Join me?

Samantha takes her arm.

38   INT. GRANDMARY'S HOUSE – UPSTAIRS BEDROOM – WEDDING DAY
*BEATRICE, Cornelia's sister, and AGATHA, Cornelia's young niece, are joined by
Grandmary and Samantha, and a DRESSMAKER. They all look at Cornelia, who is
fixing her hair.*

SAMANTHA

You look like a fairy tale.

AGATHA

Like a princess.

DRESSMAKER

Could you take this, Jessie?

*Jessie lays the veil out on the bed. As Grandmary, Samantha and Beatrice help Cornelia
with her corset, Agatha wanders over to the veil, touching it lightly.*

*Agatha sees the ladies occupied and slips the veil on her head, and turns round and round.
She screams.*

CORNELIA

Oh, no!

BEATRICE

Agatha!

THE VEIL HAS CAUGHT ON A NEARBY IRON AND CATCHES FIRE!

Cornelia rushes over to put out the flame, but the veil is singed and ruined.

DRESSMAKER

Your veil is ruined.

BEATRICE

Cornelia . . . I'm so sorry. Agatha, you could
have been hurt. Look what you did!

AGATHA
(sobbing)
I'm sorry, Aunt Cornelia. I didn't mean to—

CORNELIA

It's all right, Agatha. Don't cry . . .

GRANDMARY

Thank goodness no one's hurt.

BEATRICE

Don't cry, sweetheart. We know you didn't
do it on purpose.

CORNELIA
(trying to hide her disappointment)
It was a mistake, that's all.

Cornelia holds the veil; she really did love it.

DRESSMAKER
You can't get married without a veil.

CORNELIA
Of course I can.

Samantha leaves the room.

39   EXT. LAWN – DAY
Samantha runs from the house.

40   INT. THE BOATHOUSE – DAY
Samantha opens the trunk containing her mother's veil. She lifts it out of the box and runs with it . . . out the door and back to the house.

41   INT. CORNELIA'S ROOM – DAY
Samantha runs in with the veil. It is the most beautiful veil we've ever seen.

SAMANTHA
Would you like to wear my mother's veil?

Cornelia is stunned, and very moved. Clearly, the wedding has unnerved her a little, too. She walks over to Samantha and takes the veil. She kisses Samantha on the forehead.

CORNELIA
It's beautiful.
                 (her eyes fill with tears)
Thank you both so much.
                 (a moment to Grandmary)
Would you help me with this?

She hands the veil to Grandmary. Grandmary is very moved, both by Samantha's gift and by touching this veil that was her daughter's—and her own—wedding veil.

Samantha watches Grandmary place the veil on Cornelia's head.

42   INT. CONSERVATORY – AFTERNOON – THE PROCESSIONAL

The wedding march is played as Samantha leads the processional through several floral arches, stopping at the last where a paper bell sways over the center. The bell has two satin ribbons attached. She is followed by Beatrice, and then Agatha dropping flowers along the aisle. Jessie and Mrs. Hawkins watch from the sidelines. Gardner and his two groomsmen stand by the last floral arch, waiting for Cornelia. Tables are set in the distance for the guests.

Cornelia arrives at the aisle on the arm of her father.

43   INT. CONSERVATORY – AFTERNOON
Uncle Gard and Cornelia stand in front of the minister, Cornelia wearing the beautiful veil.

MINISTER

Dearly beloved, we are gathered together in the sight of God and the presence of these witnesses to unite Cornelia Stanton Pitt and Gardner Elliot Edwards in holy matrimony, a state first ordained by God in the Garden of Eden. Into this holy estate these two persons present come now to be joined. Wilt thou have this Woman to thy wedded wife, to live together after God's ordinance in the holy estate of Matrimony? Wilt thou love her, comfort her honor and keep her in sickness and in health; and, forsaking all others, keep thee only unto her, so long as ye both shall live?

GARD

I will.

MINISTER

Wilt thou have this Man to thy wedded husband, to live together after Gods ordinance in the holy estate of Matrimony? Wilt thou obey him, and serve him, love, honor, and keep him in sickness and in health; and, forsaking all others, keep thee only unto him, so long as ye both shall live?

CORNELIA

I will.

MINISTER
O Eternal God, Creator and Preserver of all
mankind, Giver of all spiritual grace, the
Author of everlasting life; Send thy blessing
upon these thy servants, this man and this
woman, whom we bless in thy Name; that,
as Isaac and Rebecca lived faithfully together,
so these persons may surely perform and
keep the vow and covenant betwixt them
made (whereof this Ring given and received
is a token and pledge), and may ever remain
in perfect love and peace together, and live
accordingly to thy laws; through Jesus Christ
our Lord. Amen. Those whom God hath
joined together let no man put asunder.

Suddenly, Samantha hears a sniff from Grandmary, who sits in the front row, and turns to see her crying. She understands, perhaps for the first time, that this wedding represents a loss for her, too.

44   INT. CONSERVATORY – AFTERNOON – CONCLUSION OF THE CEREMONY
Samantha has hold of a ribbon and Beatrice has hold of another.

MINISTER
I now pronounce you Man and Wife...

Beatrice nods to Samantha and they pull the ribbons.

The bell in the center of the arch bursts open and flower petals drop on the newly married couple.

Samantha watches.

Pause on a SLOW MOTION moment of pure and utter happiness for the bride and groom as they are showered with petals.

45   INT. CONSERVATORY – LATER IN THE DAY

Sam overhears a conversation between two of Cornelia's jealous friends.

> KATHERINE
> What a pleasant occasion.

> ELIZABETH
> And he's a fine catch. But then we always knew she'd marry well.

> KATHERINE
> Not so well.

> ELIZABETH
> What do you mean?

> KATHERINE
> His niece is coming to stay with them till Christmas. Poor Cornelia will have a ready-made family, less than a month after her wedding.

Samantha registers this information.

46   INT. CONSERVATORY – LATER

The crowd flanks a path of flowers that leads to the double-door exit of the room. Gard and Cornelia, in traveling clothes, run down the path as the guests cheer and throw rice. At the door, now Cornelia turns and throws her bouquet while Gard excuses himself and takes Samantha aside.

UNCLE GARD

We'll be back next month, and then we'll
have lots of wonderful adventures. How
does that sound?

Samantha smiles.

The crowd cheers off-camera as one of the guests catches the bouquet. She passes it to a guest.

UNCLE GARD

Letting Cornelia wear your mother's veil was
very generous, Samantha.

SAMANTHA

I did it for you.

UNCLE GARD
(kisses her forehead, then)

I know.

SAMANTHA

Good-bye, Uncle Gard.

Gard joins Cornelia and they leave together. Everyone's joyous—except Samantha.

48   EXT. FRONT YARD – ANOTHER DAY
Nellie is looking for Samantha.

NELLIE

Samantha . . . over here . . .

Samantha looks. Nellie jumps.

  NELLIE

                            Here . . .

Samantha walks over. Nellie produces a jar of coins.

                                        NELLIE

                            Look what I found. It's—

                                        SAMANTHA

                            NOOOOO!

                                        NELLIE

                            Yes! Eddie Ryland's money jar! I watched him
                            bully the milkman this morning, and then I
                            followed him and found his hiding place.
                                        (very proud of herself)
                            The well.

Push in to CU on Samantha's face registering it.

                                        NELLIE

                            Whatever should we do with it?

49   INT. CHURCH PEW – MORNING
      CU: A collection plate is passed.

      A choir is HEARD singing a hymn. Light streams through a stained-glass window.

      *The sound of the hymn is interrupted by the clank of coins . . . as Samantha empties the
      contents of Eddie's money jar into the collection plate. The noise is deafening. Everyone
      looks, especially Eddie, who is furious.*

                                        SAMANTHA

                            Amen.

                                        71

Samantha looks back at Nellie, who is sitting with her father and sisters in the back row. They are victorious.

49A INT. CHURCH – BEHIND THE BACK PEWS – DAY

> SAMANTHA
> I will write to you three times a day. I'm
> going to miss you so much.

> NELLIE
> I am going to miss you something awful,
> Samantha Parkington. Ya promise you won't
> forget me, now?

> SAMANTHA
> Forget you? I will be back before you know it.
> We'll spend Christmas after Christmas
> together. How does that sound?

> NELLIE
> That sounds grand!

> SAMANTHA
> I promise. Not even New York City can keep
> us apart. You'll see.

> END OF ACT THREE

ACT FOUR

50A ESTABLISH EXT. GARD'S HOUSE – EARLY AUTUMN – DAY
Gard, Cornelia, and Samantha exit a large stately home on New York City's Gramercy Park.

> SAMANTHA (V.O.)
> Dear Nellie, it's just like you said.

51 EXT. GRANDMARY'S BACKYARD – SAMANTHA'S TREE – DAY
The trees have turned yellow and red.

> SAMANTHA (V.O.)
> New York is so noisy. Even at night. And
> everyone moves so fast.

Nellie sits down with a letter. She puts a slide into the stereopticon.

SERIES OF SHOTS/MONTAGE

51A EXT. NEW YORK CITY STREET – DAY
New York streets with traffic snarled

> SAM (V.O. CONT.)
> I've never seen so many trucks and wagons
> and horses and trolleys and bicycles and
> automobiles, and I don't know how they
> keep from hitting each other.

51B EXT. NEW YORK CITY STREET – DAY
Policeman arguing with a man driving a wagon

> SAM V.O. (CONT.)
> Uncle Gard says that pretty soon they'll have to make rules that certain streets will only go one way.

51C EXT. NEW YORK CITY STREET – DAY
Image of the subway construction

> SAM V.O. (CONT.)
> They're building a train that runs under-ground—he subway, they call it. But I can't imagine why anyone would want to ride under the ground.

51D EXT. NEW YORK CITY STREET – DAY
Samantha buys chestnuts from a street vendor.

> SAM V.O. (CONT.)
> I've tried the chestnuts, like you told me to, but I like the smell better than the taste.

51E EXT. GARD'S HOUSE – EARLY AUTUMN – DAY
Samantha enters Gard and Cornelia's house.

> SAM V.O. (CONT.)
> I miss our yard. And I don't like how the houses are all stuck together. Please write soon. Love, Samantha.

51G EXT. SCHOOL – DAY

Samantha and miscellaneous teachers and school children arrive for the school day.

51H ESTABLISH UPPER EAST SIDE STREET – DAY

52 INT. SCHOOL CLASSROOM – DAY

TEACHER and STUDENTS settle in.

> TEACHER
> As soon as everyone is settled, I'd like to introduce a new student, Samantha Parkington.

Samantha manages a smile.

> TEACHER
> Who comes to us from Mount Bedford, New York, which is quite a change. Isn't that right, Samantha?

> SAMANTHA
> Yes.

> TEACHER
> Maybe you'd like to tell us a little about your life in Mount Bedford?

The teacher motions for Samantha to stand up. Which she does, reluctantly. She tries to think what to say, but nothing comes to her.

                    SAMANTHA
Well . . . first . . . Mount Bedford is . . .not a
mountain.
                   (clears her throat)
It's houses and churches and a river and . . .

The teacher tries to help.

                    TEACHER
And what river is that?

                    SAMANTHA
                  (stumbles nervously)
The Husdon. Hudson. Hudson. Sorry.

A few students giggle.

                    TEACHER
That's all right. We're all nervous when we
come to a new place. The river is the Hudson
River, the same one that runs down the west
side of Manhattan and into the ocean.

Samantha sits down, relieved.

                  TEACHER (O.S.)
Now. Who can name the longest river in the
United States?

53   EXT. RYLAND HOUSE – DAY
*Nellie finishes sweeping leaves into a pile, walks over to a little fenced in garden area, and
bends down to check the plants. She pulls paper and pencil from her pocket and starts to
write.*

With an unladylike tear in her stocking, Samantha Parkington rushes home to have tea with Grandmary, filled with the exciting news that there are girls moving in next door!

When Nellie comes to work as a maid in his family's home, pesty Eddie Ryland has someone new to torment. But Nellie and Samantha find a way to get even with Eddie.

"I could teach you to read! We could meet every day, beside the hedge. . . . It isn't hard to learn."
—Samantha

"Gardner promised me he would tell you I was coming, Mrs. Edwards. I can see that he didn't."
—Cornelia

The O'Malley sisters, played by
Hannah, Olivia, and Kelsey, wait for
their next scene.

"Star light, star bright, first star I see tonight."
—Samantha and Nellie

"I don't think the girls meant any harm."
—Grandmary

In the orphanage dormitory scene, Jenny and Bridget, played by Olivia and Hannah, wait for the cameras to start rolling and the director to call "Action!"

Once the cameras start rolling and the action starts, Olivia and Hannah have to pretend that the cameras aren't there.

The wardrobe crew is on hand to make costume repairs between takes, if needed. They use everything from safety pins and tape to needle and thread to hold things together.

"Samantha needs three sisters. And not just any three sisters. She needs you. All of you. What do you say?"
—Uncle Gard

A "stand-in," wearing modern clothes, takes AnnaSophia's place while lighting is worked out between scenes. When the cameras are ready to roll again, AnnaSophia will come back to the set.

Samantha sees an address that matches the one circled on the scrap of newspaper.

"Police! Help! Someone took my babies!"
—Mrs. Frouchy

Kelsey and AnnaSophia, between takes

"Nobody wants to know where their frocks come from, just so they keep comin'."
—Nellie

"These are not the words I had written, but they are the words I need to say."
—Samantha

"If our factories can hurt children, then we have not made good progress in America."
—Samantha

Samantha's most appreciative audience

"Oh, Grandmary, I've missed you!"
—Samantha

*"I believe it takes two to speak the truth—One
to speak and the other to hear."*
—Grandmary

Samantha's happy family out for a sleigh ride.
The green screen behind Cornelia, Nellie, and Samantha will be replaced by film of a snowy background, and the two pieces of film together will look like one realistic image.

NELLIE (V.O.)
Dear Samantha: Our pumpkins are comin' in.
I can't believe it's almost October and . . .

54 INT. CLASSROOM
As the class chatters around her, Samantha reads Nellie's letter.

NELLIE (V.O.)
Have you made many friends yet?

TEACHER (O.S.)
Good morning, class.

Samantha puts her letter away. She stands with the other students..

STUDENTS
Good morning, Miss Stevens.

TEACHER
Today I have a very exciting announcement.
The school is conducting a speaking contest
on the subject Progress in America. The
contest will take place at the Christmas program, and the winner will be announced that
evening.

Sam's head perks up; her eyes brighten.

TEACHER
You can write on a topic of your choice—
advances in medicine, transportation, anything modern and new.

A hand goes up.

EDNA
Could I write about the telephone?

TEACHER
The telephone is an excellent example.
Anyone else?

Samantha raises her hand.

SAMANTHA
Factories?

TEACHER
Another good idea. A single factory can do
the work of an entire town in one day. Think
of it! Yes, Emma?

EMMA
My uncle runs a factory. May I write on that too?

TEACHER
You all may write on anything you wish. But
only twelve speeches will be chosen. And
those chosen will be presented in front of the
entire school at the Christmas program. Your
speeches are due by Thanksgiving.

57   INT. GARD'S HOUSE – FOYER – LATE AFTERNOON
Samantha, pacing, is working on her speech. The front door opens and Uncle Gard walks in.

SAMANTHA
Products that are made by hand will be
replaced by those made by machine—
Uncle Gard!

UNCLE GARD
Hello, angel. How was school today?

SAMANTHA
It was good, thank you. I'm practicing my speech on factories. Do you want to hear it?

UNCLE GARD
(sits down)
Of course.

SAMANTHA
"Factories are the foundation of progress in America. They can make perfect products every time, and make plenty of them, too, enough for everyone all at once. They will provide jobs for everyone who wants one, too. Products that are made by hand will soon be replaced by those made by machine."

UNCLE GARD
I am impressed.

Before Gard can respond, Cornelia comes in the front door.

CORNELIA
Afternoon mail!

Samantha runs over.

SAMANTHA
Anything for me?

79

UNCLE GARD
(to Cornelia)
Hello, my sweetheart.

CORNELIA
(reading)
There is a postcard to all of us from
Grandmary. Aunt Frances is much better,
and she is going to visit with her a bit longer.
I am happy for her. She does not get to see
her sister often, I'd imagine

UNCLE GARD
(winking to Samantha)
Nor the Admiral. Who conveniently lives
nearby.

SAMANTHA
Nothing from Nellie?

CORNELIA
Afraid not.

SAMANTHA
I haven't heard from her in weeks.

Cornelia sits and continues looking through the mail.

CORNELIA
There's a letter here from Mount Bedford.
From Mrs. Hawkins.

SAMANTHA
What does it say?

CORNELIA
(reading)

Oh, dear.

SAMANTHA

What?

CORNELIA

Nellie's father has died. From influenza.

SAMANTHA

No! Poor Nellie! May I see—

Samantha takes the letter from Cornelia and sits down.

SAMANTHA

She says Mrs. Ryland has sent the girls to an orphanage.

Tears fall from her eyes as she continues reading.

SAMANTHA (CONT.)

In New York! Coldrock House. Do you know where that is? Is it near?

UNCLE GARD

It shouldn't be too hard to find.

SAMANTHA
(to Gard)

Can we go see them, Uncle Gard?

UNCLE GARD

I will get the address and stop at the orphanage on my way home tomorrow.

57A EXT. COLD ROCK HOUSE ORPHANAGE – DAY

A horse and carriage stop outside the orphanage. Gard gets out. He stops to look at the building before walking up and knocking on the door.

We move past him to the Coldrock sign above the door.

58 INT. PARLOR – EARLY EVENING

A meeting is in progress in which Cornelia speaks to a group of eight women who sit in a semicircle, listening. Samantha stands in the corner, separate from the group, listening. She is clearly unhappy.

CORNELIA

We must stand up for what we believe is right! We must make up our own minds. The time has come to change the old ways. Women must vote. The time has come for all of us to speak out. . . . And in support, Mrs. Winthrop and Mrs. Vandergeld will organize a peaceful gathering at Madison Square Park, a week from Tuesday.

MRS. VANDERGELD

Women in all forty-five states will be holding similar gatherings on that day.

CORNELIA

Then we should see great success!

Applause all around. The women start to gather their things to leave.

MRS. VANDERGELD

Very happy to have met you, Samantha.

SAMANTHA
(struggling to be polite)
Thank you. Pleased to have met you, too.

MRS. VANDERGELD
I'm always encouraged when young people join our discussions. Are you anxious to vote someday?

SAMANTHA
(polite, but firm)
I don't think so. No.

Cornelia steps in.

CORNELIA
Then she won't have to. Isn't that right, Mrs. Vandergeld?

MRS. VANDERGELD
Quite right.

CORNELIA
It's the right to vote we're fighting for, not the requirement.

MRS. VANDERGELD
Good night, Samantha.

SAMANTHA
Good night.

CORNELIA)
(*turning to Samantha*)
I hope you weren't too terribly bored.

Samantha smiles politely and watches the ladies leave.

59   INT. PARLOR –– LATER

SAMANTHA
I'm practicing my piano lesson.

CORNELIA
I'd like to stay and listen. Would you mind?

SAMANTHA
No.

Cornelia stuffs envelopes while Samantha finishes playing a piece.

CORNELIA
That was lovely, Samantha.

SAMANTHA
Thank you.

An awkward pause. Samantha gets up and sits down next to Cornelia.

CORNELIA
Would you like to help?

They stuff envelopes.

SAMANTHA
Uncle Gard told me you remind him of my
mother.

CORNELIA

I take that as a great compliment.

SAMANTHA

But Uncle Gard says you never knew her.

CORNELIA

No, but it's because I'm beginning to know
you. Anyone who had you for a daughter
would be . . . would want to spend every
minute with you.

SAMANTHA

I remember her hair. In my face when she
would kiss me good night.
(she smiles)
And I don't know why I thought of this now,
but she hated chickens.

CORNELIA
(smiles)

Chickens?!

SAMANTHA

She hated them!

They share a laugh, feeling the beginnings of a bond.

THE FRONT DOOR OPENS. Little bells ring. They get up and go to the door.

CORNELIA

It's Gard!

SAMANTHA

Uncle Gard!

61   INT. PARLOR - CONTINUOUS

Gard enters. Samantha rushes up to him. She hugs and kisses him. Cornelia takes his hand.

UNCLE GARD

Hello, ladies. Look at you two. I'd say I'm the luckiest man in New York, wouldn't you?

SAMANTHA

Did you find the orphanage?

Gard takes Samantha by the hand as they sit down. Cornelia sits as well.

UNCLE GARD

I did.

CORNELIA

Wonderful!

SAMANTHA

How is Nellie?

UNCLE GARD

Well . . . they wouldn't let me see her.

CORNELIA

What do you mean?

He leads them to the sofa. They sit down.

62   INT. PARLOR – CONTINUOUS

UNCLE GARD

The orphans are not allowed to have visitors who are not related.

CORNELIA

That's preposterous!

SAMANTHA

Why?

UNCLE GARD

Each institution makes its own rules.

SAMANTHA
(to Gard)
There must be some way that I can see her.

CORNELIA
(an idea)
Mr. and Mrs. Vandergeld donate a great deal to New York orphanages. One of these could well be Coldrock.
(pause)
Excuse me.

Cornelia leaves the room.

SAMANTHA

I should never have come to New York. If I were still at Grandmary's, Nellie and her sisters could come and live there.

UNCLE GARD

You mustn't blame yourself, Samantha.

From the hall.

CORNELIA (O.S.)
Yes? Hello? Can you connect me please to
The Vandergeld residence on Fifth Avenue?
Thank you very much.

END OF ACT FOUR

ACT FIVE

63 EXT. THE COLDROCK ORPHANAGE – THE NEXT DAY
Samantha and Cornelia walk up the steps to the orphanage. It's a forbidding, dreary building. Directly behind them, a servant carries large baskets of fruit. Samantha isn't entirely sure she trusts Cornelia. A MAID, LILIAN, follows them inside.

64 INT. THE ORPHANAGE – DAY
Samantha and Cornelia stand up as an imposing but exceedingly solicitous woman enters the room.

> MRS. FROUCHY
> You must be Mrs. Edwards. We've been
> expecting you.

> CORNELIA
> Pleased to meet you, Mrs. Frouchy.

> MRS. FROUCHY
> Mrs. Vandergeld sent word you'd be arriving.
> She spoke very highly of you.

> CORNELIA
> And of you, Mrs. Frouchy.

> MRS. FROUCHY
> Mrs. Vandergeld is our most generous benefactor.

> CORNELIA
> Would this be a convenient time for a tour?

Mrs. Frouchy gets a good look at the elegant way Cornelia and Samantha are dressed.

MRS. FROUCHY
Yes, of course. Lilian! Come with me.

One of the MATRONS shepherds a line of GIRLS through the hall.

MATRON
No speaking.
(to Cornelia)
Ma'am.

MRS. FROUCHY
I'm sure you must understand the importance
of rules for girls like this. Obedience, Order,
and Discipline. These are the things that will
enable them to find homes. Follow me.

They start up the stairs.

65   INT. ORPHANAGE – STAIRS / DORMITORY – DAY
We arrive at the top of the stairs and see the dormitory. Cornelia and Samantha are stunned
to see so many GIRLS, all looking sad and abandoned.

MRS. FROUCHY
Here is the dormitory for the younger girls.

CORNELIA
Are there always this many? It seems like
there are not enough beds.

MRS. FROUCHY
Two of the girls are leaving today, actually. To
a good home, in the country. We'll have a
party for them later.

By the looks on the girls' faces, Cornelia and Samantha both know she is lying.

Mrs. Frouchy leads them through the room. As they pass the beds, Samantha sees BRIDGET and JENNY and puts her finger to her lips.

65A INT. ORPHANAGE – SECOND DORMITORY ROOM – CONTINUOUS
They walk in the room for the older girls and Samantha immediately sees NELLIE sitting on her bed like a prisoner. She indicates to Nellie that she shouldn't acknowledge her, but Nellie already knows this, of course.

> MRS. FROUCHY
> And here we have the dormitory for the older
> girls. Nine to sixteen.

> CORNELIA
> May my niece hand out fruit?

> MRS. FROUCHY
> Yes, of course. What a lovely, well-behaved
> child.

Cornelia directs Mrs. Frouchy's attention to the far side of the room in order to distract her.

> CORNELIA
> Thank you. Now, Mrs. Frouchy . . . how many
> girls do you have in this dormitory?

Samantha walks along the row of beds on the other side of the room. She can't wait to get to Nellie, but she knows to be careful.

As she hands out fruit, the girls say "Thank you" and seem genuinely astonished that someone has come in from the outside world.

Finally, Samantha reaches Nellie. They speak furtively.

> NELLIE
>
> Samantha! What are you doing here?

> SAMANTHA
>
> Nellie! Are you all right?

Nellie shakes her head no, holding back tears.

> SAMANTHA
>
> You're so thin. And look at your hands. Here.
> Take my gloves.

> NELLIE
>
> Did you see Bridget and Jenny downstairs?
> Are they all right?

> SAMANTHA
>
> You mean you don't see them?

> NELLIE
>
> They won't let us play together. I don't know
> why. I'm sure they think I've abandoned
> them.

Mrs. Frouchy looks over.

> SAMANTHA
>
> You cannot stay here! Are you ever allowed
> outside?

> NELLIE
>
> Only when I have to dump out the ashes
> around the back. Each day at four o'clock.

MRS. FROUCHY
We must let the girls rest now.

CORNELIA
Are we ready, Samantha?

SAMANTHA
(to Nellie, frantic whisper)
I'll come and find you . . . four o'clock.
(then to Cornelia)
Ready.

66   EXT STREET – DAY
Cornelia and Sam walk down the street. Both of them are furious.

SAMANTHA
That was a horrible place. Everything was so
dirty!

CORNELIA
And that dreadful woman.
(more to herself than to Samantha)
It's as though she's punishing the children for
being orphans.

SAMANTHA
Nellie doesn't ever see her sisters.

CORNELIA
I could never have imagined such a place.
This has to change.

Samantha looks at Cornelia and considers her.

67   INT. SCHOOL HALLWAY – DAY

Several girls are putting up pictures of pilgrims and other Thanksgiving things.

Samantha comes down the hall pushing a large basket with a sign inside it. We can't read the sign yet.

Samantha takes the sign out of the box and sticks it up on the wall. Two other girls, EDNA and EMMA, watch. Both are snobby girls filled with disdain for what Samantha is doing.

EDNA

What's the basket for?

SAMANTHA

It's for coats.

EMMA

Coats go in the coat closet.

SAMANTHA

This is for coats you don't want any more.

EMMA

Why do you want our old coats?

SAMANTHA

For an orphanage. They need all kinds of things, like hats and gloves and anything warm, really. They're stuck there . . . and we need to help them.

Samantha walks away.

EMMA

Maybe *you* do.

Edna walks over toward Samantha.

EDNA

(whispering)
I have some old coats at home. They don't fit anymore. And gloves too. I'll bring 'em in tomorrow.

SAMANTHA
(sweetly)
I like your pilgrims.

EDNA
Thanks.

68   EXT – THE ORPHANAGE A FEW DAYS LATER
Cornelia and Sam walk up the steps with a large box of coats and a hamper of food.

The door is opened by THE MATRON.

MATRON
Yes, Mrs. Edwards. Mrs. Frouchy is expecting you. Let me take that box for you, ma'am.

CORNELIA
I have a hamper here full of pumpkin pies and Thanksgiving treats for the children. May we bring them into your kitchen?

MATRON
I'll take that from you. Follow me.

SAMANTHA
I'll just wait outside.

Cornelia and Sam exchange conspiratorial looks.

CORNELIA

All right.

Once Cornelia is inside, Sam runs off around the corner.

69   EXT. THE ALLEY BEHIND THE ORPHANAGE – DAY
Nellie comes out with the ashes. But she is not wearing the gloves.

SAMANTHA

Nellie! Nellie!

Nellie looks more defeated today than before.

SAMANTHA

What happened to your gloves?

Nellie dumps the ashes.

NELLIE

Mrs. Frouchy took them. Samantha, she also
took the stereopticon when we first arrived.

SAMANTHA

She stole them?
                    (timidly)
What about Lydia?

NELLIE

They'll never find her. Don't worry. She's safe.

SAMANTHA

I'm going to go in there right now and . . .

NELLIE

Please, Samantha. I don't want any more trouble. I didn't get any dinner for three days now.

Samantha pulls out rolls and cakes from her pocket.

SAMANTHA

I brought you some rolls, with cheese inside.

NELLIE

Thank you, Samantha. Mrs. Frouchy says
she'll place me out if I don't behave.

SAMANTHA

What's that?

NELLIE
(shaking her head)

Sending me out on the orphan train. To get
adopted by a family far away. Mrs. Frouchy
says girls with my training go real fast in the
farm country.

SAMANTHA

And Jenny and Bridget?

NELLIE

No, they're too young. If she sends me away,
I'll never see them again.

SAMANTHA

NO! You *cannot* go! The three of you have to
stay together. I have to think about what to
do. I'm not going to let this happen to you,
Nellie. I'm not!

70 INT. DINING ROOM – THANKSGIVING NIGHT

The table is outfitted in Thanksgiving regalia. Gard, Cornelia, and Samantha sit in their places, served by Gertrude.

> UNCLE GARD
>
> Did you know, Gertrude? Our Samantha was chosen out of all the girls at school to speak at the Christmas program.

> GERTRUDE
>
> Isn't that wonderful!

> SAMANTHA
>
> It's not just me. There are twelve of us.

> UNCLE GARD
>
> But I will see only you.

> SAMANTHA
> *(she laughs)*
>
> Uncle Gard.

> CORNELIA
>
> That is quite an accomplishment to be one of the twelve, Samantha.

> UNCLE GARD
>
> It is a shame that Mother won't hear it.

> CORNELIA
>
> Then Grandmary will have the pleasure of hearing only Samantha when she returns.

Gertrude brings over the turkey. Everyone applauds.

UNCLE GARD
Beautiful. Our first Thanksgiving!

SAMANTHA
(looking around)
I wish that everyone had all the blessings that
we have tonight.

Cornelia holds her hands out indicating that they say grace.

CORNELIA
Shall we?

Pull back as they bow their heads.

CORNELIA/GARD/SAMANTHA
Father, we thank thee for this food, for health
and strength and all things good. Amen.

71 EXT. THE ALLEY BEHIND THE ORPHANAGE – DAY
It's cold outside. You can see the air coming out of Nellie's mouth.

*She wears a thin coat tightly wrapped around her. Her stockings are tattered. She dumps
the ashes and blows on her hands.*

SAMANTHA (O.S.)
(hushed whisper)
Nellie.
                    (a little louder)
Nellie!
                    (Nellie turns.)
Come on. Everything's ready. We need to
hurry.

NELLIE

What? What are you talking about?

SAMANTHA

Look, if we don't go now, we never will.

NELLIE

Go? Where?

SAMANTHA

With me. I'm taking you all.

NELLIE

Now?

SAMANTHA

Right now. What's wrong?

NELLIE
(a very small voice)

I'm scared.

SAMANTHA

It'll be all right. Go get Bridget and Jenny and
I'll meet you in front of the coat closet. I'll
meet you there in five minutes.

Nellie stands, frozen still.

SAMANTHA

GO! NOW!

Nellie looks at her for a moment, then puts her bucket down and . . . she's off, through the
back door, without another word.

72   INT. COLDROCK ORPHANAGE – HALLWAY – CONTINUOUS
P.O.V.: Nellie

The Matron holds a large wad of bills. She turns to Mrs. Frouchy, giving Nellie the opportunity to sneak upstairs.

> MATRON
> I'll deposit the donation money Monday,
> Mrs. Frouchy?

Mrs. Frouchy eyes the bills.

> MRS. FROUCHY
> Best give it to me. I'll hold on to it.

The Matron is dubious.

> MRS. FROUCHY
> For safekeeping.

Nellie races up the stairs, unseen.

> MATRON (O.S.)
> (subservient)
> Yes, ma'am.

72B INT. UPSTAIRS HALLWAY
Nellie (who clutches her Lydia doll), Jenny, and Bridget sneak down the hallway. Nellie hurries her sisters along.

> NELLIE
> Come on, girls, we have to go now!

72C INT. STAIRWAY/FOYER
P.O.V.: Nellie

As Nellie comes down the stairs she sees the Matron on her way to answer the door. Nellie motions for the girls to follow and creeps down one step at a time when she hears:

> MATRON (O.S.)
> Who is this? What are you doing here?

> SAMANTHA
> I came to bring donations. For the girls.
> I usually come with my aunt, who's very
> good friends with Mrs. Vandergeld.

With the Matron's back to her, Nellie seizes the opportunity to run into the office, just as the Matron turns. Samantha, watches, trying not to react.

> SAMANTHA
> We usually just leave the boxes beside the
> coat closet.

> MATRON
> Fine! Off you go.

> SAMANTHA
> Thank you.

72D INT. FRONT OFFICE/CLOSET
Samantha pulls coats out from the box.

> SAMANTHA
> *(frantic whisper)*
> Nellie? Where are you?

Nellie peeks out of the closet. Bridget squeals from happiness at seeing Samantha, but Nellie claps a hand over her mouth.

SAMANTHA
(*whispering*)
Quick. Take one. For the girls, too. Now put them on. Good. Let's go.

BRIDGET
Samantha!

They're about to leave when they hear:

MRS. FROUCHY (V.O.)
I'm just going to put the money in my safe . . .

Samantha pushes them back in the closet. But Bridget is across the room. Nellie gestures for her to get down.

Suddenly, Mrs. Frouchy bursts into the front room. She closes the door, takes the money out, and counts it. She removes a picture from the wall, and begins working the combination on the safe. We hear it click open. She puts the money inside, perhaps placing a few dollars down the front of her dress. She then closes the safe, spins the combination and hears:

BRIDGET SNEEZES.

Mrs. Frouchy turns on her heel.

MRS. FROUCHY
What in—

She sees Bridget, and then three other figures unrecognizable in coats and hats.

MRS. FROUCHY
What? Who are you?

Bridget trips Mrs. Frouchy. Mrs. Frouchy lands on the floor.

Nellie bursts out of the closet, grabs Bridget.

> NELLIE
>
> Bridget! Come!

Samantha takes Jenny's hand.

> SAMANTHA
>
> RUN!

> MRS. FROUCHY
>
> No, you don't. Stop! Wait! Help!
> (screaming)
> Evelyn! Someone! Help! Stop them!

72F INT. FRONT HALLWAY

The girls burst in from the office and head to the door as fast as they can run.

Nellie runs with Bridget by the hand. Mrs. Frouchy is gaining on them.

> MRS. FROUCHY
>
> Stop! Thief!

But they are gone.

She follows them outside.

75 EXT. STREET – CONTINUOUS

Samantha runs as fast as she can down the street with Jenny. Nellie pulls Bridget along. Mrs. Frouchy and the Matron run into the street after them.

> MRS. FROUCHY
> Police! Help!

A POLICEMAN comes over.

> MRS. FROUCHY
> Someone took my babies . . .
> *(a beat)*
> and the donation money.

The Matron reacts.

> MRS. FROUCHY
> All of it. Over two hundred dollars.

The policeman reacts.

> POLICE
> Don't you worry! I'll get 'em.

And he runs off after Samantha, Nellie and the younger girls.

Samantha leads the girls down the street. The policeman follows at a run.

P.O.V.: Policeman: the girls disappear down a busy street.

END OF ACT FIVE

ACT SIX

76   EXT. GARD AND CORNELIA'S HOUSE – LATE AFTERNOON
Gertrude walks past. Samantha signals.

Nellie, Bridget, and Jenny rush up the stairs to the attic.

77   INT. THE ATTIC – LATE AFTERNOON
Samantha opens the door and lets the girls in. The late-afternoon sun comes in the attic windows, making shadows fall across the room.

There are stacks of blankets and pillows, piles of books and clothes.

There is also a table set for four. Jenny runs for the table.

> BRIDGET
> *(shouting)*
> Dinner!

> NELLIE
> Bridget! Be quiet! If we get caught we'll get in trouble, and so will Samantha's family.

> BRIDGET
> Why can't we live here?

> NELLIE
> *(gently)*
> We're wards of the state. That's what Mrs. Frouchy calls us. We belong to them.

> BRIDGET
> To the state?

NELLIE

Yes. And if anyone finds us here, they'll be
made to turn us in. So you must be quiet,
now. Do ya understand?

Bridget and Jenny, a bit terrified, nod.

SAMANTHA

It's all right for now. Eat up. There's turkey
and dressing and cranberries . . .

*Nellie and Samantha exchange glances. Nellie's eyes say "Thank you." Samantha's say
"You're welcome."*

SAMANTHA

I put pajamas on the bed.

NELLIE
(whispers)
How did you get all this up here?

SAMANTHA

I told Gertrude it was for a family in need.
(a moment, then brightly)
And it is.

NELLIE

It's so nice and warm.

We hear the front door opening from downstairs.

SAMANTHA
(hearing a noise)
Oh no! They're home. I have to go down to
dinner. I'll try to come up after.

NELLIE
How can I ever thank you?

Nellie grabs her and they embrace.

SAMANTHA
You're my friend. That's what friends do.

79 INT. GARD'S HOUSE – HALLWAY/VESTIBULE – EARLY EVENING
P.O.V.: Samantha::

Samantha overhears Gertrude mid-conversation with Mrs. Frouchy.

GERTRUDE
Samantha's been here all afternoon.

MRS. FROUCHY
Are you certain?

GERTRUDE
(calls)
Samantha?

Samantha ducks behind a door and answers lightly.

SAMANTHA
Yes?

GERTRUDE
(satisfied)
Any further questions?

MRS. FROUCHY
(cutting her off)
My matron informed me that she was at the
orphanage a short while ago. A few of my
girls have since gone missing along with
two hundred dollars.

GERTRUDE
What are you implying?

MRS. FROUCHY
If I find that she has been involved, I'll report
her to the authorities.

GERTRUDE
You'll not make threats here. Good day. I said
good day.

Gertrude closes the door on Mrs. Frouchy. Samantha scurries up the stairs.

79D INT. ATTIC – NIGH

*Samantha and Nellie sit quietly. Bridget and Jenny sleep. Nellie is wearing the pajamas
that Samantha left for her.*

NELLIE
Do you think she knows?

SAMANTHA
I am not sure. She said she would go to the
police and that we took money.

NELLIE

That is a terrible lie! Oh, Samantha, I don't want you to get into any trouble on my account. I'm going to find a job as soon as I can, so we can get a room of our own.
              (Nellie looks very confident)
Someone will hire me.
              (her confidence begins to fade)
I miss my Da.

SAMANTHA
              (hugging Nellie)
Don't worry, Nellie, I'm not going to let anything happen to any of you. I promise.

80   INT. DINING ROOM – LATER

The evening meal is almost over. Uncle Gard, Cornelia, and Sam sit at the table. Gertrude serves. Samantha tries to look relaxed.

CORNELIA
Mrs. Vandergeld has installed a shower.

UNCLE GARD
Passing fancy.

SAMANTHA
Like a rain shower?

CORNELIA
Exactly. Only it is inside the house, and you stand under and the water falls.

UNCLE GARD
A ridiculous contraption.

CORNELIA
Absurd.

UNCLE GARD
Prone to breaking, I'm sure.

CORNELIA
I'm sure.

UNCLE GARD
(winking to Samantha)
And you'd like one, I suppose?

CORNELIA
Absolutely!

Uncle Gard pulls a letter out of his pocket.

UNCLE GARD
It's from Grandmary.
(to Samantha)
She's been to see the Admiral!

Samantha smiles.

CORNELIA
What's so amusing?

UNCLE GARD
The Admiral's been proposing to Mother
twice a year for a dozen years, I'd say.

CORNELIA

No wonder she thought we were rushing
things.

SAMANTHA
(standing, stretching)
May I be excused?

CORNELIA

Of course, dear. I'll be up to tuck you in.

Samantha leaves. Gard watches her go.

SAMANTHA

Good night, Uncle Gard.

UNCLE GARD

Good night, Samantha.
(quietly, to Cornelia)
Gertrude had a visitor today. Mrs. Frouchy.

CORNELIA

Mrs. Frouchy from the orphanage? What did
she want?

GERTRUDE

Hard to say, madam. But it seemed to me she
was accusing our Samantha of stealing.

CORNELIA

Gard, we must do something to stop this
woman.

UNCLE GARD

I agree.

82   INT. SAMANTHA'S ROOM – NIGHT
Samantha sits at a writing desk.

CU Samantha's hand as Samantha writes a letter.

> SAMANTHA (V.O.)
> Dear Grandmary, it's almost Christmas and
> I can't wait to see you.

83   INT. DINING ROOM – NIGHT
Gertrude leaves as Samantha scoops up rolls,butter, and other items.

> SAMANTHA (V.O.)
> Cornelia and I are making our own
> ornaments for the Christmas tree.

84   INT. ATTIC – NIGHT – LATER
Samantha unpacks a pillowcase full of food .

> SAMANTHA (V.O.)
> And making cookies and fruitcake and even
> plum pudding, though I'm not sure we did it
> right.

85A INT. STAIRWAY – NIGHT
Samantha creeps up the stairway with a bottle of milk and a loaf of bread.

> SAMANTHA (V.O.)
> Since Nellie is in New York now, all that's
> missing is you.

87   INT. ATTIC – A FEW DAYS LATER – DAY

Bridget is lying down on her blanket, pale and sick looking. She coughs, again and again. Jenny puts down her doll and goes to Bridget. She pats her hand, then picks up a glass of water and offers it to Bridget. Then Jenny leans her head down to Bridget's face, and pulls away quickly, feeling that Bridget is very hot. Jenny hugs her. Bridget doesn't respond.

87A INT. UPPER HALLWAY – DAY

Jenny creeps out the door and down the steps after Gertrude has passed..

Jenny creeps past the room where Cornelia sits and approaches Samantha's door.

88   INT. SAMANTHA'S ROOM – DAY

SAMANTHA

Jenny! What are you doing down here?

Jenny grabs her hand.

SAMANTHA

Is something wrong? What's the matter?

Now Samantha sees that Jenny really senses some danger.

SAMANTHA

What is it? All right, I'll come with you.

Jenny drags Samantha out the door and up the stairs.

89   INT. ATTIC – DAY

They enter the room. Samantha takes one look at Bridget and sees that she is sick.

SAMANTHA
Bridget? Are you all right? You're so hot.

Bridget coughs. Samantha puts her hand to Bridget's forehead. It is burning up.

SAMANTHA
Burning up. Can you drink a little water?

Samantha holds the glass up to Bridget, but she can't drink any. Samantha takes off her apron and wets it with the water. She bathes Bridget's face in the water.

SAMANTHA
I have to get you help. Do you know where
Nellie went? Was she looking for a job?

Samantha looks at the newspapers on the floor. She sees a circle around a GIRLS WANTED ad.

SAMANTHA
(to Jenny)
Is this where she went?
(realizes)
You don't know, I know. All right. You keep
putting cold water on Bridget's face. Like
this. I'm going to go find Nellie. All right?

Samantha rushes out the door and down the stairs.

90   EXT. A LOWER EAST SIDE STREET OF FACTORIES – DAY
Holding the paper, Samantha walks down a street unlike any she's seen in New York.

The buildings are factories, the people are dressed in whatever they have, and the air is gray and choked with smoke. People stand around fire barrels on the street keeping warm. It feels like we've gone back in time. There are holes in the pavement, and some streets are not paved. Men come out of buildings carrying rolls of fabric or rolling carts of coats and dresses.

Samantha is too stricken to even speak. But she sees an address that matches the one circled on the scrap of newspaper.

Samantha opens the door and confronts a stairway that seems to lead up and up forever.

90A EXT. A LOWER EAST SIDE FACTORY

Samantha arrives at the top of the stairs. She looks in the grimy window and is horrified. Machines are whirring away, but the place is filthy, and so are the PEOPLE working there. It's all CHILDREN, or seems to be. It is cold, without heat. You can see the breath coming from people's mouths.

A girl from the stairway arrives and pounds on the door. A skinny man (FACTORY MAN) comes to the door and lets her in with a key. He stops Samantha.

> FACTORY MAN
> You want a job, put your name on that list. If
> you can't write, make an "X." Then get in line
> behind them.

She turns to see a line of children aged seven to sixteen, in air so cold you can see their breath. They huddle together, waiting. Suddenly we hear:

> YOUNG BOY
> Owwwww. Owwww! My finger. It's stuck!

The man runs over.

> FACTORY MAN
> Worthless brats. Hold on there. If the needle
> breaks, it comes out of your pay!

Then he roughly helps the YOUNG BOY.

> YOUNG BOY
> Owwwww.!No, please. Stop! Stop.

FACTORY MAN
Quiet! Ahhh, no. The needle broke.

A WOMAN goes over and offers the boy a rag. She helps him up.

FACTORY WOMAN
(to boy)
Here, wrap your finger. Keep pressing on it
hard.

The boy, shaking and crying, makes his way out of the factory. The Factory Man goes to the front of the line.

FACTORY MAN
We've got an opening now!

A YOUNG WOMAN replaces the young boy. Samantha steps out of line and walks up to the Factory Man.

SAMANTHA
Excuse me, sir. Sir! I'm looking for my friend.

FACTORY MAN
This ain't a tea party. You wanna see your
friend, wait till seven o'clock.

SAMANTHA
No sir, I can't wait. It's an emergency. There
she is.

Samantha gestures and calls out.

SAMANTHA
Nellie! Nellie! Come quick.

Nellie stands up from her machine.

FACTORY MAN
Leave the machine, lose the machine. Them's
the rules.

SAMANTHA
Bridget is sick!

FACTORY MAN
(to Nellie)
You decide, girlie. You leave now, you don't
come back.

Nellie leaves. The Factory Man goes to the next person in line.

FACTORY MAN
We got a machine empty here! Next!

91   EXT. LOWER EAST SIDE STREET – DAY
They hurry along the street.

NELLIE
What's the matter with Bridget?

SAMANTHA
I don't know. She's hot. I should've just told
Cornelia. I don't know—

NELLIE
No, you did the right thing. Let me take a look
first. Could just be a sore throat. She gets those.

SAMANTHA
Why didn't you tell me what factory work
was like?

NELLIE
Nobody wants to know where their frocks
come from, just so they keep comin'.

SAMANTHA
Are all factories like that?

NELLIE
All the ones I've seen.

SAMANTHA
The books don't tell this part of it.

NELLIE
Then the books are wrong. Let's run.

The girls start to run.

92 INT. ATTIC – LATE AFTERNOON
Jenny sits with Bridget, who is now gasping for breath. The window is open, but Bridget is still as hot as can be.

NELLIE
She's burnin' up, Samantha. I've never
seen her this bad. She didn't look right
this morning. It's my fault for leavin'.

SAMANTHA
It's getting so cold up here.

She makes a decision.

NELLIE
Where you goin'?

SAMANTHA

To Uncle Gard and Aunt Cornelia.

NELLIE

You can't!

She looks to Bridget.

SAMANTHA

I have to.

Samantha walks back out the door.

93   INT. PARLOR – LATE AFTERNOON
Samantha steps into the room. Uncle Gard and Aunt Cornelia are reading.

UNCLE GARD

Hello, angel. The big day is coming, isn't it?
How is your speech? Are you nervous?

CORNELIA

I can't wait to hear it all the way through.

SAMANTHA

I need to talk to you . . . both.

Cornelia looks to Gard.

UNCLE GARD

We're listening.

SAMANTHA

I did something wrong, and I need some
helps Nellie's sister, Bridget, is sick. Upstairs.

CORNELIA/UNCLE GARD

Upstairs?

94   INT. GUEST ROOM – LATER

Bridget lies in a fluffy featherbed. A DOCTOR attends to Bridget. Cornelia and Gertrude stand by.

DOCTOR

She's quite dehydrated. Under my orders, you're not to move her for at least a few weeks, until she gets her strength back.

CORNELIA

Of course, Doctor.

95   INT. PARLOR – CONTINUOUS

Gard, Nellie, Samantha, and Jenny sit quietly as Cornelia and the doctor enter.

UNCLE GARD

Any improvement?

CORNELIA

Not yet. The girls are all to stay here until the patient recovers.

Samantha and Nellie exchange looks.

DOCTOR

I'll be back in the morning to check on her.

CORNELIA

Thank you, Doctor.

GERTRUDE
I'll see you out.

The doctor leaves.

CORNELIA
(to the girls)
Gertrude's made up beds for you in
Samantha's room. You go on up now. I'll go
and sit with Bridget.

Nellie is about to go with Jenny, but then she turns to Cornelia.

NELLIE
Samantha brought us here to save me from
being sent on the orphan train, without my
sisters.

CORNELIA
They're not supposed to separate families!

NELLIE
They do a lot of things, ma'am, they're not
supposed to. Good night. And thank you for
your kindness.

Nellie leaves with Jenny.

UNCLE GARD/CORNELIA/SAMANTHA
Good night, Jenny; good night, Nellie.

SAMANTHA
I'm sorry, Uncle Gard, Aunt Cornelia.

UNCLE GARD

You can't break the law, Samantha, even
when a law seems unfair.

SAMANTHA

I had no choice.

UNCLE GARD

You always have the choice to come to me.
You know that.

SAMANTHA

But you don't even want *me* here; why would
you want three girls who aren't related to
you.?

UNCLE GARD

Who says we don't want you here?

SAMANTHA

Aunt Cornelia's friends.

CORNELIA

My friends?

SAMANTHA

At the wedding. They said it was a shame
that I was coming here.

CORNELIA

Oh, Samantha! Don't think for a minute that's
how I feel. They were just jealous, and mean,
and petty. You're our family, Samantha. I
want you here.

SAMANTHA

Yes, Aunt Cornelia.
                    (turning to leave, then turning back)
No one touched Mrs. Frouchy's money.

UNCLE GARD

We know that.

SAMANTHA

Please don't make Nellie go back. They can't
go back there.

UNCLE GARD

I have no alternative. I must inform the
authorities that they are here.

SAMANTHA/CORNELIA

Right now? This late?

UNCLE GARD

I'll wait until morning. But I have no other
choice.

*Suddenly, not knowing where else to go, Samantha runs to Cornelia and grabs her around
the waist.*

SAMANTHA

No!

END OF ACT SIX

ACT SEVEN

96 INT. ORPHANAGE OFFICE – ANOTHER DAY
Mrs. Vandergeld sits across the room from Mrs. Frouchy.

> MRS. FROUCHY
> Would you like some tea?

> MRS. VANDERGELD
> No, thank you. I'll be brief.

> MRS. FROUCHY
> Before you speak, I'd like to say that we're
> not going to press charges on the Parkington
> girl, as long as she returns the money she
> took.

> MRS. VANDERGELD
> She claims she didn't take it.

> MRS. FROUCHY
> *(continues, oblivious)*
> With Christmas coming, we may have to rely
> once more on generous benefactors such as
> yourself. We don't want to disappoint the
> children—

> MRS. VANDERGELD
> No, we don't. Which is why, Mrs. Frouchy,
> we're replacing you.

> MRS. FROUCHY
> What? You're what?

MRS VANDERGELD
The Board of Directors is unhappy with the
way you've been running Coldrock. It was
never our intention to fund a prison. And
there have been indications for a good while
that funds have been misappropriated.

Mrs. Vandergeld eyes Mrs. Frouchy's new hat and mink cape.

MRS. FROUCHY
You simply can't be serious!

MRS. VANDERGELD
Oh, yes. I *simply* can. Good day!

96A INT. ORPHANAGE
Cornelia greets Mrs. Vandergeld on her way out of the room, their complicity clear as day.

99 INT. SCHOOL AUDITORIUM – DUSK
A large crowd of parents and friends cheer a speaker as she returns to her seat. Samantha and eleven other GIRLS sit ON STAGE. The last girl is finishing. The PRINCIPAL waits.

EMMA
Factories will produce many goods at the
same time, most economically. Everyone can
work there. And that's why factories are the
golden future of America.

The crowd applauds and she returns to her seat.

PRINCIPAL
And the final speaker will be Samantha
Parkington.

Samantha walks to the podium.

IN THE AUDIENCE, Gard and Cornelia are watching with pride. Directly in front of them we see Grandmary and a distinguished-looking man with something distinctly nautical about him.

ON STAGE

> SAMANTHA
>
> Americans are very proud of being modern.
> We are proud of our progress. We are proud
> of the machines in our factories, and the
> products they make. But Americans are
> proud of being truthful, too. Last week I went
> to a factory, and what I saw was nothing like
> what I had been told.

The TEACHER looks angry.

> SAMANTHA
>
> There were children, younger than I am,
> working from early morning until after dark.
> They were dirty, they were cold, and they
> couldn't leave. They don't have time to go to
> school and they are too tired to play.

The teacher approaches the stage. Samantha stands taller, straighter, with more conviction about her cause.

> SAMANTHA
>
> Children are hurt in these places. I know I
> saw one. If our factories can hurt children,
> then we have not made good progress in
> America.

Samantha looks to Cornelia.

> SAMANTHA
> These are not the words I had written. But are the words I need to say.

Cornelia's eyes are full.

> SAMANTHA
> Americans are good and kind. And good and kind people take care of children, even if they aren't their own. When we do that, we can truly be proud of our factories and our progress. Thank you."

Samantha stops, curtsies, then heads back to her seat.

Cornelia and Uncle Gard stand and applaud.

Others begin to join in.

100 INT. RECEPTION HALL – SAME
Cornelia and Gard embrace her.

> UNCLE GARD/CORNELIA
> We're so proud of you! That was great!

Now Samantha sees Grandmary and ADMIRAL BEEMIS.

> SAMANTHA
> Grandmary! You were here?
> (she turns to Cornelia)
> Did you know they were coming?

CORNELIA
We wanted it to be a surprise.

Samantha flies across the room and into Grandmary's arms.

GRANDMARY
Samantha, you were magnificent! How did
you know about factories?

SAMANTHA
Nellie told me. And then I went to get her,
where she worked and—

GRANDMARY
This was very brave of you.
(*her manners reappear*)
Forgive me. You remember Admiral Beemis?

SAMANTHA
Very nice to see you again, Admiral.

ADMIRAL BEEMIS
Your speech was very impressive, Samantha.
No wonder your grandmother talks about
you all the time.

The teacher approaches. She is not very happy.

TEACHER
Samantha, that speech was not the speech
that you entered in the contest.

SAMANTHA
I changed it after I saw the truth.

TEACHER

I'm afraid you've been disqualified from the competition.

CORNELIA

Disqualified? For telling the truth?

Grandmary gives the teacher one of her regal stares.

GRANDMARY

She won me over. And I'm a much tougher judge, I can assure you. I believe it takes two to speak the truth—one to speak and the other to hear.

The teacher backs off.

TEACHER

I beg your pardon.

GRANDMARY
(to Samantha)
Your mother would have been proud of you today, Samantha. We are all quite proud of you, too.

Samantha beams and takes Grandmary's hand.

101 EXT. STREETS OF NEW YORK – LATE DAY
Samantha, Gard, and Cornelia ride back to the house in an open carriage. Bells are jingling.

UNCLE GARD
How do you feel, Samantha?

SAMANTHA
I feel that Gertrude is overworked.

The adults are amused and confused.

SAMANTHA
Which is why she's so slow.

CORNELIA
Slow?

SAMANTHA
She needs help.

Uncle Gard and Aunt Cornelia have finally caught up with her.

UNCLE GARD
Cornelia, you've created a crusader.

SAMANTHA
After all, it's a very large house for one
person to keep.

UNCLE GARD
And how many more maids do we need?

SAMANTHA
Three.
                    (smiling)
At least.

CORNELIA
Which is really four, counting Gertrude.

SAMANTHA
Besides, if I come to visit more often . . .

UNCLE GARD
What do you mean, if you come?

SAMANTHA
You're going to need more help. I'm a
handful!

They laugh. Then he gets serious and takes her hand.

UNCLE GARD
Samantha, Cornelia and I were hoping that
you'd like to come stay here with us.

CORNELIA
Permanently.

Samantha looks at them, realizing that they're not kidding.

SAMANTHA
You mean leave Mount Bedford? For good?
But what about Grandmary? I wouldn't want
her to be all alone.

UNCLE GARD
She won't be alone. Because . . . Grandmary
has finally decided . . .

SAMANTHA
(gleeful)
NO!

UNCLE GARD
Yes. She has accepted the Admiral's proposal.

CORNELIA

. . . which is why we hoped you'd consider staying with us.

Samantha is speechless.

UNCLE GARD

What do you say, Samantha? Will you adopt us?

SAMANTHA

Will I? Yes.

They embrace.

102 INT. GARD AND CORNELIA'S HOUSE – CONTINUOUS

Samantha, Gard, and Cornelia walk into the living room. Samantha gasps with joy. The tree is gorgeous. Underneath are piles and piles of presents. Grandmary, Admiral Beemis, Nellie, and Jenny are there.

SAMANTHA

Oh! It's so beautiful! Who did all this?

GERTRUDE

I did, miss. With a little help.

Angle on Nellie.

SAMANTHA

I've never seen a prettier tree in my whole life.
          (leading Gertrude toward a chair)
You're probably worn out. You should rest. Really. Save your strength.

GERTRUDE

I'm fine.

Uncle Gard is smiling. Gertrude looks at Samantha as if she's crazy.

SAMANTHA

Can we open the presents now?

GRANDMARY

No!

UNCLE GARD

No. Not until tomorrow. But you can start working on your notes to Santa.

CORNELIA

And I believe there is hot chocolate in the kitchen. Gertrude?

Samantha pulls Uncle Gard down to speak to him.

SAMANTHA

Does Santa know that Nellie and her sisters are here?

UNCLE GARD

Believe me, Samantha, Santa knows every-thing.

103A   INT. THE FIREPLACE – LATER THAT NIGHT

A Christmas Eve moment! Samantha, Nellie, and the girls, in nightgowns, put their notes for Santa at the fireplace. They hang their stockings and place milk and cookies just so.

They then check on the large hampers in the corner. Cornelia supervises.

GRANDMARY

What's all this?

SAMANTHA

For the orphanage.

ADMIRAL BEEMIS

Quite a bounty.

UNCLE GARD

This is nothing. Cornelia's arranged for a
whole Christmas feast tomorrow. She's got
half of New York donating presents and food,
and clothes, and . . .

GRANDMARY

Can I help?

CORNELIA

Yes, of course.

104A   INT. SAMANTHA'S ROOM – NIGHT – LATER
Jenny is asleep. Nellie and Samantha sit in the window seat, wrapped in blankets.

SAMANTHA

Isn't it amazing that we can be here, together?
This is my favorite Christmas Eve, Nellie.

NELLIE

I wonder where we'll be next Christmas.

SAMANTHA

Let's make a wish.

135

SAMANTHA
Up there someplace is our wishing star. Make
your wish, Nellie. Close your eyes tight.
(both girls do)
And wish with all your might. Wish like
you've never wished before.

NELLIE
I'm wishin', Samantha.

They hold hands, with eyes closed.

NELLIE
(whispering)
I'm wishin'.

104B   EXT. GARD AND CORNELIA'S HOUSE – MORNING
We hear the sound of jingling bells, then . . .

105   INT. SAMANTHA'S ROOM – MORNING
Bridget walks in and Samantha wakes up. Nellie and Jenny are up.

NELLIE
I knew you would have a good sleep.
(to Bridget)
Bridget! You look good! How do you feel?

BRIDGET
I'm better.

SAMANTHA
Merry Christmas, Bridget.

Cornelia comes into the room.

CORNELIA

Merry Christmas! Bridget, how's our patient?

Cornelia goes over to Bridget.

BRIDGET

Hungry.

CORNELIA

Let's go have Christmas.

They race downstairs to a magical wonderland of Christmas.

107 INT. PARLOR – CHRISTMAS MORNING

The beautiful tree glitters, the stocking are stuffed. Hot cocoa is ready. Everyone is there, including Grandmary and the Admiral.

Gard takes the little girls' hands and calls them all to him.

UNCLE GARD

Wait. Before you start screaming at all the
silly things Santa has left in your stockings,
we have something to tell you.

SAMANTHA

Uncle Gard . . .

Cornelia takes Samantha's hand. There's something in this that reassures Samantha.

UNCLE GARD

Samantha asked us if you three girls could
come here and be maids.

NELLIE
Oh yes, sir. We will work very hard. Morning
to night, sir.

UNCLE GARD
But we do not need any more maids.

Nellie looks dejected.

UNCLE GARD
However, Samantha is going to be living here
with us permanently. Did you know that,
Nellie?

NELLIE
Yes, sir.

UNCLE GARD
And there is one thing she needs that we
would very much like to give her.

NELLIE
Yes, sir.

CORNELIA
She needs three sisters. And not just any three
sisters. She needs you. All of you. What do
you say?

NELLIE
(beaming)
Oh, yes!
        (turns to Samantha)
Sisters, Samantha.

SAMANTHA

Sisters.

Nellie and Samantha hug.

Aunt Cornelia comes to hold Uncle Gard's hand.

UNCLE GARD

Aunt Cornelia and I want all four of you to be our girls. To live here and grow up together in this house as one family. Would you like that, Bridget?

BRIDGET

Oh yes.

UNCLE GARD/AUNT CORNELIA

Jenny?

Nellie starts to talk for her.

NELLIE

Jenny says—

JENNY

Jenny says "yes, sir."

Gard sweeps Jenny up in his arms. She gives him a little kiss on the cheek. The girls all run to hug Gard.

Samantha goes to Cornelia and embraces her. Gard catches sight of this.

UNCLE GARD

That's my girl.

And we pull back to see the family celebrating their first Christmas.

139

107A EXT./INT. COLDROCK ORPHANAGE – CHRISTMAS DAY

Cornelia and Samantha, climb the steps of Coldrock House, carrying Christmas hampers and gifts. The door opens and they are greeted by the new head of the orphanage, the kindly MISS THOMAS, and several happy children. They go inside.

As the door closes, snow begins to fall gently.

108 EXT. PARK – A SLEIGH ON A WINTER'S DAY

THE FIRST SNOW OF THE SEASON BEGINS TO FALL ON . . .

THE NEW AND EXPANDED EDWARDS FAMILY, WITH GRANDMARY, ARE IN A SLEIGH, UNDER BLANKETS, LAUGHING AND ENJOYING THE HOLIDAY SEASON.

                    NELLIE
        First snow, Samantha. Do you think we're
        dreamin'?

                    SAMANTHA
        If we are, I hope we never wake up!

                    THE END